INFORMAL INTRODUCTION

"Good afternoon of importance to discu

"Is she expecting

Proper etiquette ...ap-pointment, which co ...into the wrong hands. Even if it didn't, depending on the status the receiver strove to maintain, a response might take a week or more.

As I reckoned the birdlike crone knew what color drawers her ladyship had donned that morning, I said, "No, there simply wasn't time to—"

"Then whatever you're selling, young lady, the missus doesn't need it."

My palm held the oak door at bay. "J. Fulton Shulteis hired me this morning to act on Mrs. LeBruton's behalf. I think if you tell her that, she'll agree to see me."

The door swung wide. Bony fingers clamped my upper arm and yanked me inside. "Lord above, why didn't you say so before the whole neighborhood got a look at you?"

"From her sharp descriptions to her crisp dialogue, Ledbetter tickles the jaded palate of any reader."
—Colorado Reverie

Praise for Suzann Ledbetter's *North of Clever*

"The colorful prose and farcical action in this cozy keep the pace moving at the speed of a magician's hand."
—Publishers Weekly

A Lady
NEVER
Trifles
WITH
THIEVES

SUZANN LEDBETTER

POCKET BOOKS
New York London Toronto Sydney Singapore

This book is a work of fiction. Names, characters, places and incidents are
products of the author's imagination or are used fictitiously. Any
resemblance to actual events or locales or persons, living or dead, is
entirely coincidental.

An *Original* Publication of POCKET BOOKS

POCKET BOOKS, a division of Simon & Schuster, Inc.
1230 Avenue of the Americas, New York, NY 10020

ISBN: 0-7434-5747-1

First Pocket Books printing May 2003

10 9 8 7 6 5 4 3 2 1

POCKET and colophon are registered
trademarks of Simon & Schuster, Inc.

For information regarding special discounts for bulk purchases,
please contact Simon & Schuster Special Sales at 1-800-456-6798
or business@simonandschuster.com

Interior design by Davina Mock

Front cover illustration by Dan Duffy

Printed in the U.S.A.

ACKNOWLEDGMENTS

Writing a novel is purported to be an isolated occupation. Au contraire. I'm blessed with a whole herd of literary Lamaze coaches, without whom this book wouldn't have been birthed.

My thanks in a huge way to: Judy Sieger; Paul W. Johns, who believes in me no matter how much I snivel; Ellen Wade, R.N., Saint of Hopelessly Kiboshed Bank Accounts and superb emergency collator; Ellen Recknor, my twin separated at birth by a few years and six hundred miles or so; Susan Fawcett, who keeps my rear in gear, more than she realizes; the fantastic crew who helped me move across the street from myself in the midst of perpetrating the enclosed murder and mayhem; and especially to Christina Boys, my smart, ever-patient and supportive editor; and to Robin Rue, agent extraordinaire and then some.

For Judy Sieger, for who you are and all you do.

ONE

The explosion hurled me backward a good five yards. It was surely a new record, though I'd never kept track of such things.

Pure luck landed me in the vegetable garden instead of the rose bed. The last time I experimented with nitrostarch, Won Li, my Chinese patron, had to fetch a ladder and pluck me from the leafy arms of an elm tree.

Splinters fell like rain from the mare's tail clouds drifting above. I was just noticing how closely the embers resembled fireflies when an explosion of a different nature erupted.

"Josephine Beckworth Sawyer!" Won Li screeched my full name in practiced, perfect English. A singsong litany of Chinese obscenities commenced forthwith.

If God were merciful, He'd have allowed Rose Mary Sawyer to live long enough to properly christen her newborn daughter. Since Mama took her last breath at the same instant I drew my first, Papa was left to his own devices. To be sure, and no pun intended, Deputy Marshal Joseph Beckworth Sawyer hadn't conceived of fathering a baby girl.

After all, from the night he and Mama wed, they'd followed to the letter the granny-woman's advice for fetching a boy. My mother had slept with a knife under the mattress and was careful not to store any skillets under the bed. For his part, Papa had sat on the roof near the chimney for seven hours, which was believed to ensure the birth of a son.

The granny-woman later blamed the hammer he'd taken with him to pretend he was fixing the roof for ruining her augery and said he was lucky I hadn't been twins. Lord only knows what poor Papa would have done had there been two of me.

Although stretching Joseph to derive Josephine made a certain kind of sense, it unfortunately brought forth images of dairy cows and vapid twits enamored of sausage curls and hair ribbons. A schoolmarm once suggested shortening the Beckworth at center to Becky, which might be fine for a sunny dispositioned, freckle-faced lass but didn't append well to a black-haired, olive-complexioned child who learned to shoot, skin, and cook her own supper by the age of eight and wouldn't have played with dolls had a dagger been held at her throat.

In the manner of counted blessings, I was told Papa would have tacked on the preordained "Junior" had the granny-woman not intervened. Truth be told, I wouldn't have minded that as much as being called Josephine, until my mouthful of a name got whittled down to the plainer, more palatable Joby.

Won Li was still chattering in Chinese when I gained

my feet. "I may not savvy your lingo, old friend," I said, "but cussing is cussing and no proper way to address a lady."

I shook clumps of tomato pulp and mud from my faded calico skirt. My white cotton waist was already scorched and chemical-stained from previous mishaps. Peeking between my lashes at Won Li discouraged further comment—from me, anyway.

Agitation inflamed the scar that welted his scrimshaw face from temple to jawbone. The disfiguring souvenir of our first meeting measured his mood like a barometer: the redder it became, the nearer he was to apoplexy. Or homicide.

"You are not a lady," Won Li said. He pointed at a blackened, smoldering patch of yard. Beyond it, neighbors peered from behind their privies and woodpiles. "You are a menace."

"A scientist," I corrected. "A student of criminality, botany, and chemistry and the only female detective on this side of the Mississippi River."

He smirked. "Then to solve the mystery of the missing toolshed, standing over there less than three minutes ago, should not tax your faculties unduly."

I favored him with an engaging smile. "Don't be silly. As you can plainly see, most of the walls are laying in the Matlocks' pasture, and I'm almost certain the door came to rest beside Mrs. Flegle's chicken coop."

The roof may have accounted for the showering splinters, but a detective deals in facts, not idle speculation.

Won Li's mouth flapped like a hooked trout. He was seldom at a loss for words, but my pyrotechnic experiments had silenced him on numerous occasions.

The simple truth is, I was born clever, and the passage

of twenty-two years had not dulled my wits. To my ever-lasting chagrin, however, those of the male persuasion admire a more practical kind of genius. A gift for darning socks with no knots in the heels, for instance.

"Simmer down, Won Li." I threaded my arm through his to steer him toward the house. "A pound of twopenny nails and some shingles will fix the shed as good as new. I'll hire a carpenter after my morning appointment and pay Jimmy Matlock six bits to scavenge around the field for our tools."

"His mother will never allow it. She has not forgotten your testing the sleeping powder on him."

"Well, it isn't as if I *forced* it on the boy. The effect wore off after three or four hours—no harm done atall."

I bunched my skirt to step over a shovel and the head of a pick, both divested of their handles. "Besides, Mrs. Matlock asked me a while back if she could buy some Morpheus powder to stir in her husband's coffee at suppertime."

Won Li glowered at me.

I laughed. "No, of course, I didn't. For heaven's sake, will you ever give me credit for the sense God gave a goose?"

He dodged the question in his usual fashion. "If I may be so bold, might I ask with whom you have an appointment this morning?"

"J. Fulton Shulteis."

"The attorney."

"Yes," I confirmed, as though J. Fulton Shulteises ran the city streets in packs, like dogs.

Won Li disengaged his arm to reach for the screen door's handle. "You cannot continue this charade forever."

"I shouldn't need to much longer. I am making quite a reputation for myself, you know."

"Ah, yes, Joby," he said. "You most assuredly are."

Whether destiny or doom guided Won Li's and my first encounter twelve years ago depended upon which of us was asked. My recollection of it is as vivid as the day it happened.

One dogwood-spring afternoon, a half dozen of the yahoos that Ft. Smith, Arkansas, drew like flies to fresh dung took exception to a Chinaman breathing the same air they did. They surrounded him, each in turn landing a wallop that sent him lurching into another fist.

I chanced upon the melee just as a thug bludgeoned the Chinaman with the butt of his revolver. In a tick, I was on the brute's back like ugly on a hog. I kicked. I screamed. I bashed the miscreant's ears with the heels of my hands.

When one of his cronies tried to pry me off, I cocked my knee and slammed a boot heel smack-center of his groin—the word, area, and essential components of which I was supposed to be ignorant. The blow not only rendered the bully unfit for a second intervention, it discouraged the others from having a go at me.

The sight of a ten-year-old, fifty-pound child—and a girl, at that—defending the defenseless shamed spectators into calling a halt to the fracas. While the thugs swaggered away to a saloon to wet their whistles, I helped their victim to his feet.

His eyes were nigh swollen shut. Blood pulsed from the gash on his cheek, his nose, and foamed his lips, yet he managed to stammer, "You ah vely blave."

I shook my head. "I just can't hash cheaters, bullies, or drunks. From what I saw, you flushed up a whole covey of them."

I took him to our cabin to cleanse his wounds. In

slurry, pidgin English, he introduced himself and said he owed me his life—a debt that must be repaid in kind or by forfeiting his own.

I didn't understand much of what he said, or what was meant by it. To me, Won Li was like a wounded puppy to fuss over and talk to while my father was gallivanting around The Nations arresting killers, thieves, and bad Indians.

When Deputy Marshal Joe B. Sawyer returned to find a battered, thirty-year-old Chinaman living in our root cellar, Papa had what could only be described as a jumping cat fit. Months passed before he was convinced that Won Li's intentions toward me were honorable to the extreme.

Providence hasn't yet seen fit to thrust me into a life-threatening situation from whence my guardian angel could rescue me. I'd often wondered if Won Li would leave when that day came; even more so this past year, since Papa's heart gave out midway between Ft. Smith and the new life we'd planned for ourselves in Denver City.

If—when—it did, I knew there'd be no fanfare. No tearful good-byes, promises to write, or visitations. He'd just roll his meager possessions in a blanket and set out before dawn broke across his back.

It was pure selfish to pray that day never came. But I did.

At the stroke of ten, I strolled into the stark front office on Larimer, midblock between F and G Streets. The clerk, a bespectacled rabbit of a man, glanced up from a ledger, then attempted to cover the page with his forearms.

"Good morning, Percy."

"It was, yes." He wricked sideward to look past me, at the door.

"Would you be so kind as to announce me?" I said. "I don't want to keep Mr. Shulteis waiting."

"But the appointment was with—"

"I'm sure you have more important things to do than argue with me." I tapped the edge of the ledger. "Such as posting that due bill to William F. Parker."

Percy started, then slammed the book shut. In his haste to exit the chair, he barked a shin on an open drawer. Limping badly and wheezing through clenched teeth, he waved a command to follow him.

I hid a grin behind my hand. Poor Percy. My ability to read upside down had never set well with him. I sensed he was the type some mothers would dote on and fathers would try to interest in blood sport.

Percy rapped once on the thick oak door dividing management from labor. At the muffled Yes? from within, he wrenched the knob and motioned me past.

I nodded my thanks and glided onto a field of plush, Aubusson ivy vines and ferns; the carpet's pattern was so lifelike a snake would feel quite at home.

"You again?" Lawyer Shulteis inquired from behind a mahogany desk as large as a buckboard's bed.

"Always a pleasure to see you, too, Fulton."

He steepled his fingers. "And what has detained your illustrious father this time? Surely he's recovered from pneumonia by now. Or was it dyspepsia?"

I took a chair that hadn't been offered. It aggrieved me the way Papa's health had suffered since his demise, but it couldn't be helped. Neither Shulteis nor anyone else in Denver City would knowingly hire a woman detective.

"Mr. Sawyer sends his most sincere apologies, but he's investigating a train robbery for the Kansas Pacific."

The attorney's jowled face reflected skepticism. "I've

done quite a bit of work for them myself. Odd, I haven't
heard of any holdups in the vicinity of late."

My belly fluttered. I clenched wads of navy bombazine
in my fists to compose myself.

When circumstances warrant, any female of Southern
extraction—present company included—institutes one of
the most potent weapons in her arsenal: the coquettish
sigh. "Maybe that's because Papa is in the wilds of southwest Kansas, although where, exactly, I have no idea."

Which was as true as gospel. I simply declined to mention the grave with his name carved on a pair of crossed
slats beside a wagon road. I couldn't have if I'd wanted to,
lest the grief rise up and devour me. Silly as it was, running the agency in Papa's stead cheated death in an odd
sort of way. A comfort, it was—particularly those nights
when I cried myself to sleep.

"I can't say I'm displeased with Mr. Sawyer's results to
date," Shulteis said, "but to the best of my knowledge, no
one in town has ever laid eyes on the man."

"All the better for a private investigator, wouldn't you
say?" I forced a smile. "Especially for one with such an
able assistant."

Shulteis cleared his throat. "Yes, well . . ."

A folded sheet of foolscap sailed across the desk. "If you
think your father would be interested, one Penelope LeBruton is seeking proof of her husband Rendal's adulterous
behavior before she proceeds with a bill of divorcement."

I tried not to let disappointment show in my expression. So far, I'd hung out to dry three wayward spouses at
Shulteis's behest. I'd hoped he had something less tedious
for me this time. Profitable as adultery could be for the
wronged party, his or her lawyer, and a detective, I
yearned for a kidnapping, or an embezzler to outwit.

"Mrs. LeBruton wants the evidence as quickly as possible," Shulteis said.

I tucked the paper into my reticule. "She'll have it."

The attorney curried his muttonchop sideburns. "How can you be so sure, with your father, as you said, '. . . somewhere in the wilds of southwest Kansas'?"

"Now, Fulton. Sawyer Investigations hasn't failed you yet, has it?"

August at the South Pole—much less the parched prairie where gold-fevered pioneers built Colorado's first boomtown—would be too warm for a bombazine suit. I hadn't a dry stitch on by the time I'd walked from Shulteis's office to the agency's headquarters at the corner of H and Champa.

Propping the door with a brick aired the stifling office a bit, but also let clouds of clay dust boil inside from horses, freight wagons, and buggies trafficking up and down Champa.

An hour's worth of envying the attorney's richly appointed workspace had reminded me that people admire Thoroughbreds for their beauty and mules for their character. As offices went, Sawyer Investigations was definitely a mule. The single room was about the size of a boxcar. Cracks in the dingy plaster walls resembled photographic negatives of an electrical storm. Bewhiskered snouts often poked through gaps in the warped floorboards.

The space was functional but a far cry from the handsome, wood-paneled den of justice I'd envisioned when Papa had announced the new enterprise at supper one evening.

I flinched at the memory of his resignation from duty. For nine infuriating months, he'd waited for President

Grant to realize the stupidity of appointing William Story, a gotch-eyed, sidewinding carpetbagger, to preside over the Federal Court for the Western District of Arkansas in Van Buren.

For the sake of argument, Joe B. Sawyer was no candidate for a halo. Those who knew he bent the law a time or ten dozen during his twenty-three years' service said he ranked a thin notch above the outlaws he captured.

Others criticized him for not turning in his badge after my mother died, as his job took him from our home in Ft. Smith for weeks at a time. It *was* hard on me boarding with this family and that one while he was gone. Now and again, I missed him so terribly, I tried my level best to hate him, but dang it all, I loved him, admired him, and respected him too much for such nonsense to embitter me for longer than an hour or so.

Down to my bones and deeper, I was proud of my father and prouder still to be Joseph Beckworth Sawyer's daughter. Papa never lied to me. He treated me like an equal. He believed I'd hung the stars and the moon but didn't shy from heating my backside with a hickory switch if the situation called for it.

Funny, how those who condemned him as a father never once asked my opinion. I reckon my growing up healthy, strong, and mostly happy was thought to be a fluke of nature, akin to the Methodist preacher's oldest daughter owning the fanciest bordello in Little Rock.

But whether a saint, a sinner, or somewhere in between, Papa had no stomach for kowtowing to a thieving judge or his flunky, Federal Marshal Logan Roots. Before roosters crowed the dawn of April 22, 1870, Papa, Won Li, myself, and a wagonload of worldly goods were aboard a ferry pointing toward the Arkansas River's west bank.

Denver City was chosen by process of elimination. Papa said Missouri was too near our native state in terrain, attitude, and number of shootists fawnching to put more holes in him than a berry sieve. Texas was a second cousin to hell on earth, with Oklahoma and Kansas Territories being firsts. California was too far removed, and Papa would sooner leave Arizona and New Mexico to the rattlesnakes and Apaches.

My thoughts on starting a detective agency weren't solicited, but the idea gave me the hooray kind of goose bumps. Denver City's renown as the Queen City of the Plains sounded classy, lively, and large—three adjectives a blind man wouldn't affix to Ft. Smith, Arkansas.

Hindsight says I was too busy imagining the miracle of sneezing in the mercantile without a neighbor lady bringing a mustard plaster to the house to notice Papa was straining to catch his breath. I don't know for certain when he passed. He rode slumped in the saddle, for quite a spell, as if he were napping before his body canted sideward and slid to the ground.

I'll hear that *thump* till the day I join him and Mama on the other side. I don't remember what came after, but the second morning after Papa's burial, Won Li said he had no choice but to tranquilize me with a gill of poppytea. He'd carried me from the gravesite, which I'd refused to leave, to a pallet he'd fashioned in the back of the wagon. The next I knew, the purple-blue peaks of the Rocky Mountains were spiking the horizon.

I'd have died of melancholy and sunstroke if Won Li hadn't intervened: thus he'd saved my life and should have been shed of his obligation. He not only disagreed, he was hugely insulted by my assumption, and went about as though I were invisible for nigh onto a week.

"A darned peaceful seven days it was, too," I said as I unpinned my flowered and feathered straw hat. It looked more fetching on the office's hat rack than it did on my head. Having been raised as ungoverned as a weed, I doubted I'd ever get accustomed being trussed from tip to toe in ladylike foofaraws.

Loosening the topmost jacket buttons saved me from strangulation without exposing my ample charms. After chucking my gloves and reticule in a bottom drawer, I commenced the daily chore of feather dusting the red grit from the massive oak partner's desk.

The owner of the secondhand store had told me two speculators had hauled it all the way from Georgia. Scars, ink splatters, and alligatored shellac had cheapened the price, as had the gouge on one side from an original owner's attempt to saw it in half after a disagreement with his partner.

The storekeeper had warned me, "I won't sell it to you unless you promise me one thing. When the day comes you want rid of it, you gotta swear you'll burn it, bust it up for kindling—I care not what—long as you don't lug it back here. I already done bought and sold that monstracious ugly sumbitch five, mebbe six times and I don't never want to see it agin in this life, nor the next."

The old coot took me for my word. For ten dollars cash money, plus six bits delivery, he threw in two high-backed swivel chairs, a pair of fancy upholstered parlor ones, a hat rack, and framed portraits of Washington crossing the Delaware and Napoleon with his hand stuck in his coat, scratching his belly.

I'd arranged a secretary's accouterments around the blotter on my side of the desk. On the other was the morning edition of the *Rocky Mountain News*, an ash receptacle with a half-smoked cigar, a bottle of whiskey, and other tokens of manly occupation.

For the longest time, I'd fooled myself into believing I'd decorated what would have been my father's realm only for show. As the window lettering said SAWYER INVESTIGATIONS, DEPUTY U.S. MARSHAL JOSEPH BECKWORTH SAWYER (RET.), PRINCIPAL, visitors would be mighty curious if they didn't see or smell a trace of the old lawdog in charge.

Now just because my mother had gypsy blood doesn't mean I believe in séances, haints, or any of that voodoo claptrap, but one evening it came to me as clear as water that Papa was leaned back in his chair. The newspaper was open across his knees, and that nasty cigar was crotched between his fingers.

There must be barbers in heaven, for his salt-and-pepper hair and beard were trimmed and combed. The trail dust had been brushed from his hat and boots; his shirt and trousers were laundered and pressed.

He couldn't have looked more at home in our parlor in Van Buren. I took it for a sign he admired seeing his name spelled out in gilt on the window and countenanced my carrying on without him.

If I hadn't let my mind drift, the clamor of footsteps on the floorboards wouldn't have given me such a start. Two expensively dressed gentlemen of middle age gandered about the room as though I were a part of the furnishings.

"Is Mr. Sawyer in?" asked the taller one. His voice was reedy, and his nose and cheeks flushed, in the mode of one regularly exposed to sunlight or liquid corn.

"Not at the moment." I walked around the desk to return the feather duster to its drawer. "Perhaps I can be of assistance?"

The shorter, heavyset man asked, "When do you expect him back?"

"I'm sorry, but I really can't say. Mr. Sawyer doesn't hold to clocks and calendars." I nodded at the parlor chair beside the desk and its twin alongside Papa's. "I'm Mr. Sawyer's assistant and would be happy to take down the particulars of your case."

They exchanged vexatious glances. "Mr. Sawyer came highly recommended," said the taller, "but this is a matter of urgency. We cannot afford to wait—"

"Then the sooner I'm apprised of the situation for Mr. Sawyer's review, the better. Wouldn't you agree?"

Grudgingly, he introduced himself and his companion. The names were as familiar as yesterday's newspaper.

Garret McCoyne was a banker and had inherited several parcels of prime Denver City real estate. The shorter man, Avery Whitelaw, owned silver mines and stamp mills that extracted gold and silver amalgam from crushed quartz.

Wealth and influence weren't their sole commonality. The McCoyne and Whitelaw households had recently been burglarized by a bold and very cunning thief.

With no evidence of forcible entry at either home, it was presumed their second-floor windows had been breached by means of a rope with a grapple attached at one end. Hooking a chimney corner, cupola, or other sturdy rooftop amenity would be pattycakes for an experienced cracksman. In each instance, the thief stripped a pillow of its case and absconded with a fortune in jewelry, including Mrs. McCoyne's renowned diamond-and-ruby tiara.

What use one might have for such a geegaw I couldn't fathom, but a quarter newspaper column had been devoted to Mrs. McCoyne's nervous prostration from which she might never recover.

The police were stymied. The McCoynes and Whitelaws were absent from their homes at the time of the intrusions. Their servants had neither seen nor heard a disturbance. None of the jewelry had surfaced as yet.

The burglar would strike again. As William Somerville said in his poem, "The Lucky Hit," "So in each action 'tis success that gives it all its comeliness." The sole questions were, Who would the thief target now? and When?

Criminitly, how my palms did itch. What a boon it would be for Sawyer Investigations to capture him in the act and recover the loot. Which I'd be delighted to do, except how should I know which Denver City mogul would be robbed next? The answer to *when* was a slightly less nebulous *soon*.

McCoyne said, "Should Mr. Sawyer deign to make an appearance, tell him Mr. Whitelaw and I will return tomorrow afternoon at two."

My eyes flicked to Papa's chair. "There's every chance he will, gentlemen. I'll be sure to give him your message."

After they took their leave, I fanned myself with the accounts ledger. Thirty-six dollars and seventy-three cents was all that separated me from destitution. Bills were mounting atop the desk. The rents were almost due on the office and the house.

The agency's till would not be vastly enriched by the fee nicked from J. Fulton Shulteis's charges for dissolving the LeBruton maritals. Somehow, by early tomorrow afternoon, I must produce a flesh-and-blood father, or McCoyne and Whitelaw would take their business elsewhere.

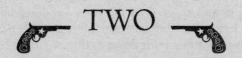

TWO

"Much as I appreciate your thoughtfulness, Won Li, you needn't bother to bring my dinner every day."

"It is no bother, Miss Joby. To bank the cookstove, harness the horse, hitch the buggy, and venture out in the midday heat is a humble servant's greatest pleasure."

I laughed. "Humble servant, my rear end. Why not admit you come here every day to spy on me, and be done with it?"

"You are most impertinent."

"I'm also right."

For once, he didn't rise to the bait. Some people enjoy trading postage stamps or mint coins as a hobby. Won Li and I swapped jibes.

"The appointment with Lawyer Shulteis," he said. "He made good on his threat never to speak to you again?"

The remark stemmed from my arrest for prostitution

three months earlier while investigating another spouse who'd cleaved onto others at every opportunity.

Shulteis explained to the magistrate why I'd been dancing on Madame Felicity's bar when the police raided the bordello. The charge was dropped, but Shulteis deducted five dollars from the agency's fee for his trouble. He'd also sworn he wouldn't acknowledge my existence if we passed on the boardwalk. As for Won Li, I couldn't recall ever seeing him so angry. Over the years, I endured hundreds of his lectures on comportment. More often than not, the lamp wicks would burn down to threads before he'd run out of steam and banish me to my bedchamber like a child.

"Fulton is an attorney by profession," I said, stifling a grin. "He lies like a rug when it suits his purposes."

Won Li's arms raised to chest level and braced like a cigar store Indian's. "Need I ask what the case for which he obviously hired you entails?"

"Nope."

"You promised you would never engage in that type of work again, Joby."

"I most assuredly did not. I promised I'd never pass myself off as a bride of the multitudes again."

My fingers were crossed behind my back at the time, but what Won Li didn't know wouldn't put his pigtail in a swivet.

"I am not one to butt into your business—"

"No, you aren't. When you meddle, you throw your whole body into it."

I bit my tongue a moment too late. Won Li bulled up as stony as a statue. I was a head taller, but he had the rare kind of dignity that sawed lesser humans off at the knees.

"I'm sorry, Won Li." I laid a hand on his shoulder. He

didn't shrug it off. "Why you didn't string me up years ago, then cut the rope a minute short of mortal, I'll never know."

His mouth crooked a nonce, the closest he ever came to a bona fide smile. "The thought has occurred to me."

"It will again."

"Of that we can be sure." He bowed at the waist. "I leave you to your dinner and will return for you at four o'clock."

He scuttled forward. The iron gray braid dangling from his shaved crown to his waist ticked like a pendulum.

"Ummm . . . Won Li?"

"Yes?"

"Could you make that half past five?"

"As you wish, Joby."

I frowned. Blind obedience was not his strong suit. "You aren't even going to ask why?"

He didn't so much as glance back at me. "A wise man does not ask a question unless certain he wants to hear the answer."

With that, he was gone.

The roast beef, steamed vegetables, and particularly the angel cake were delicious. I was hungry, but I picked at more food than I consumed. The office was simply too hot and sultry for a full noonday meal.

Studying the city directory between bites didn't aid digestion, either. Like a gambler perusing a racing form for a horse with a serendipitous name, number, or color, my finger descended the listings as though the cosmos would identify the burglar's next victim.

It would have been easier to predict which house was prone toward a lightning strike. Everybody knows, a flue without a wisp of smoke purling forth is in peril. Lightning is drawn to cookstoves, but never one with a fire burning in it.

Dirty utensils and dishes stowed in the basket, I gloved my hands and repinned that boulder of a hat on my head. Much as I admired Denver City, its womenfolk were sticklers about social convention. A cyclone ripping the town to hell and gone might excuse a lady appearing in public sans proper accessories, but something as piddling as heat stroke would not.

The boardwalks teemed with a splendid display of democracy in motion. Upturned crates supported three-card monte and chuck-a-luck games for the convenience of those who preferred to lose a week's wages in the great outdoors. Millionaires tipped silk top hats to shopgirls in homespun bonnets and gingham dresses. Wealthy matrons and Jezebels alike were decked out in the latest Parisian fashions, which enraged the former and amused the latter.

Ragtag street vendors hawked, "Apples! Fresh apples!" "Cee-gaaars!" "Roaasted pea-nutsss" and "Raaazors, scissors, knives to grind." Weary cowboys with dirt-creased necks and saddlebags slung over a shoulder yearned for a hot bath, a shave, and a cold draught beer—in that order.

Hollow-cheeked consumptives, wanting desperately to believe that altitude stayed the Grim Reaper's call, shuffled alongside working stiffs of every nationality and creed. Unbeknownst to them all, a fast-wilting female detective cleverly disguised as a slender, blue-eyed, young lady of modest means and temperament was in their midst.

The clang of a horsecar's bell was a sore temptation. Admission to the steel-railed trolley only cost five cents. I couldn't divine a cheaper luxury, but my purse was too thin for mollycoddling. A disciple of Benjamin Franklin's "a penny saved is a penny earned," I was not, yet a nickel couldn't be spent but once.

Why hadn't I asked Won Li to wait and drive me in the buggy? An excellent question, answered by the prospect of basking in his tacit disapproval all the way across town and back.

His chauvinism was selective. It applied to no one, save me. After Papa died, turning tail for Ft. Smith held no appeal for Won Li or myself. Before we arrived in Denver City, he indulged my talk of soldiering on with the agency. Won Li presumed it to be a tribute to my beloved father, which I'd jettison when the shock of Papa's death relaxed its grip on my heart.

Realizing I was not only stone serious but a born detective rankled the liver out of my patron. He'd encouraged my childhood ambitions to become an actress, then an alchemist, and later, an archaeologist. It never occurred to him that private investigation conglomerated all three.

The difference between Won Li and my father was that Papa prayed my realms of interest didn't portend life imprisonment, even though incarceration would let him know where I was and what I was doing at any given moment. As for Won Li, he refused to accept my disinterest in attending medical school or pursuing a college professorship. The occupational totem pole his dreams had carved with my likeness ranked "female detective" so low, I'd have to look up to see solid ground.

The day the agency opened for business, I was full of starch and vinegar. I made a deal with the old devil: If Sawyer Investigations went bankrupt, I'd set my sights on a medical career. Won Li was too honorable to bet against my success, but there was nothing in our agreement about cheering me on.

Lo, if he had any idea how few nickels separated my dream from his, he'd be posting letters of inquiry to the Eclectic Medical College, Women's Medical College of Pennsylvania, the Boston Female Medical College, and the University of Michigan.

The LeBrutons' scarlet hibiscus bushes and my face were the same shade of aflush upon my approach to their block stone home. A broad veranda wrapped the front and bowed gracefully around a bay-windowed turret. White lace curtains frothed the windows, uncommonly large, sashed affairs for a city where winter came early and stayed on like a shirttail relation down on his luck.

The front screen was unhooked. An ancient Negress in a gray dress answered my second pull on the vestibule's bell cord. Her flint expression telegraphed displeasure with my impatience. I chastised myself for provoking her.

Maids' and butlers' attitudes in delicate household matters were always suspect. Sympathetic as they might be to their mistress, their salaries weren't paid from her purse.

"Good afternoon, ma'am," I said. "I have a matter of importance to discuss with Mrs. Penelope LeBruton."

"Is she expecting you?"

Proper etiquette required a note requesting an appointment, which could easily fall into the wrong hands. Even if it didn't, a response might take a week or more, depending on the status the receiver strove to maintain.

As I reckoned the birdlike crone knew what color drawers her ladyship had donned that morning, I said, "No, there simply wasn't time to—"

"Then whatever you're selling, young lady, the missus doesn't need it."

My palm held the oak door at bay. "J. Fulton Shulteis hired me this morning to act in Mrs. LeBruton's behalf. I think if you tell her that, she'll agree to see me."

The door swung wide. Bony fingers clamped my upper arm and yanked me inside. "Lord above, why didn't you say so before the whole entire neighborhood got a look at you?"

The maid's abrupt change in demeanor was as disconcerting as it was welcome. She ushered me to a hall bench and sat me down. "You wait here whilst I see if Miz Penny's up to a visit. If she isn't, I surely am. One way or t'other you and ol' Abelia will have us a talk in the back kitchen, directly."

Before my wits were about me, she'd rounded the stairway's newel post and was two steps from the landing. I wrenched sideward and called, "Tell her Joby—"

"Hush your mouth, girl. What I don't know, I don't have to lie about later."

Dread wrapped my shoulders like a cloak. From the minimal information Shulteis had given me, I'd assumed this was a typical case of a wife punishing her husband's philandering where it would hurt him most: his wallet.

Abelia treating me like an answer to a prayer countered that: moreover, fear had flashed in her eyes when she'd stopped me from giving my name.

I heard her rap softly on a door. "It's just me, Miz Penny," she said, her voice as sweet as a mother crooning to an infant.

I hugged my reticule to my bosom and surveyed the oak-paneled reception hall. Ferns on tall stands graced the corners. An imposing grandfather clock ticked like a snare drum in a funeral cortege. As if made for it, a carved, walnut secretary with a drop-front desk and glass doors fit the nook between a nickel-plated stove and the archway to the front parlor.

Everything from the marble-topped table with its silver salver for calling cards to the fringed lampshades, Brussels carpets, and gilded ceramic bric-a-brac bespoke . . .

Props. My lips curled over my teeth. Scenery arranged as if for a lyceum stage play. This was not a home, much less a happy one—a fact intuition would have provided even if I'd been ignorant of the owners' marital strife.

I started when Abelia said, "Get yourself up here and be quick about it. Can't never tell when that man'll take a notion to sashay home."

The carpet runner muffled my sprint up the stairs. Five of the doors exiting off the gloomy landing were closed. Near the sixth, Abelia's stooped figure was silhouetted by a slash of wan sunlight. "Wait for me here in the hall after Miz Penny speaks her peace," she whispered as I passed by.

Was Mrs. LeBruton enfeebled? An invalid? Ye gods and good Christmas. What manner of stewpot had J. Fulton Shulteis gotten me into this time?

When I entered the room, the sensation of falling into a cloud dazzled me. Plush white carpet swallowed my walking boots to their uppers. Innumerable yards of gauze-white fabric swagged the pale blue walls like bunting, draped the bay windowed alcove, and festooned the bed's canopy.

It seemed perfectly natural for a tiny, blonde angel in a lacy bed jacket to be reposed against mounds of fluffy pillows. The bruise shadowing her right eye and raw scrape at her left cheekbone were anything but.

"J. Fulton Shulteis is a shyster of the first rank," she said in a velvety drawl, "but he is unquestionably discreet. I trust you shall be, as well."

"Nothing you say will leave this room, Mrs. LeBruton."

"Including that I have decided not to proceed with the divorce?"

My eyes averted to her abraded cheek. A cupboard door wasn't the villain. Nor would a fall scuff one side of her face and contuse the other. I'd witnessed and participated in enough schoolyard brawls to recognize a backhanded ring mark when I saw one.

It wasn't my place to tell her a *divorce a mensa et thoro* was an alternative. Such a decree leaves the marriage intact but bars a spouse from bed and board, whereas a *divorce a vinculo matrimonii* ends the legal relation.

Contrary to other contracts, the marital variety can't be dissolved by agreement of the parties involved—only by judicial authority.

Mrs. LeBruton continued, "A note was delivered to Mr. Shulteis an hour ago, instructing him to forgo the bill of divorcement. Abelia insisted I tell you in person."

I glanced sideward. Abelia's gaze telegraphed a plea to extend my discretion to her.

It was a waste of breath, but I said, "May I ask why you changed your mind?"

Her response was so long in coming I'd ceased to expect one. "Have you ever been married?"

"No, ma'am."

Her hint of a smile was that of a wistful martyr. "Only after a woman has been wed for a while can she understand what is meant by the bonds of holy matrimony."

Abelia muttered under her breath. I sincerely doubted it was "amen."

"I appreciate the courtesy you've shown me, Mrs. LeBruton. Should anyone inquire, I have never had the pleasure of making your acquaintance."

The brittle reserve vanished from her lovely porcelain features. She slumped against the pillows. "Thank you. Perhaps someday we will meet under less trying circumstances."

"I truly hope we do."

I gently closed the door behind me, though I damn well wanted to slam it hard enough to rattle the windowpanes. Why in God's name would any woman stay shackled to a man that beat her? Did Penelope believe the rice powder caked under her eyes hid his monogram? Is that why she hadn't bothered to blame clumsiness for her injuries?

That's how Janey Lou Bakker always explained it when she'd slunk into the mercantile in Fort Smith with a split lip or her eyes blackened and nigh swollen shut.

"My man Harley says I'm surefooted as a hog on ice," she said so many times she should have embroidered it on her dressfront to save wind. "Law, I cain't scratch my head and fry sidemeat what it don't portend a calamity."

Townsfolk shook their heads and murmured that Harley would kill her someday. He did, and a vigilante posse hanged him for it, the night after they served as pallbearers at Janey Lou's funeral.

Abelia slipped from the bedchamber like a wraith. She held a finger to her lips and pointed to an adjacent door. I followed her down the backstairs to the kitchen.

The room smelled of cinnamon, yeast rolls, and a ham baking in its own pot liquor. Bunched herbs were pinned to the white cotton curtains above a spacious, granite sink and the hand-pump that served it. Glass-paned cupboards boasted everyday dishes enough to serve an army. Solid-doored cabinets below the counters would hold all the needed pots, pans, kettles, and tins.

"I been caretaking Miz Penny since she was twelve year old," Abelia said. "Her daddy owns a steamship line out San Francisco way. Rich as King Midas and didn't get that way being kind."

She paused, then muttered, "That dear, sweet girl jumped out of the frying pan and into the fire. I told her and told her, LeBruton was cut of the same cloth as her father, but would she listen? Ain't her fault she don't know what love is. Mine and her mama's is all she's ever had."

With a grunt, Abelia whisked an envelope from the butcher-block worktable. Prying up a stove lid, she flung the envelope into the fire. The clank of the lid resettling in its groove was as irrevocable as a gunshot.

When she turned, her eyes were red-veined, but dry. "If it's the lastest thing I do on this earth, I'll get Miz Penny away from that son of Satan she married."

"Was that her note to Mr. Shulteis?"

"Oh, you're a quick one, I'll give you that." Abelia fetched a glass from a cabinet. "Miz Penny didn't have no choice but write it." Lemonade was dispensed from a jug stored in the icebox. I whimpered at the sight of it.

"When she told Mr. Rendal she'd had enough of his bedding every slut that cocked a hip at him, he slapped her." The glass banged the table in front of me. "He said he'd married Miz Penny for her money and that she'd do as she was told, or he'd have his friend the judge declare her insane and lock her up in an asylum."

Hatred radiated from the old woman's very pores. She knew how easily Rendal LeBruton—or any husband— could dispose of a troublesome wife, then quietly divorce her and take her wealth as his own. It didn't happen every day, but often enough to be common knowledge.

I sipped at the cold, lemony-sweet ambrosia, though I

wanted to gulp it in a single swallow. Declining a plate of molasses cookies, I asked, "Then why did you burn the note, Abelia?"

"Because Miz Penny can't lie worth spit. This way, she don't have to. For all she knows, it went to that shyster, like she was told."

"But her husband is bound to find out it didn't. I can't act as Shulteis's agent knowing his client believes she's fired him. What happens if Shulteis serves LeBruton with notice of the dissolution? Fulton has put the cart before the horse, when the respondent was a known philanderer."

The last remark prompted a mental smite to the forehead. On the eve of our first collaboration, Won Li said Shulteis was rumored to have warned a captain of industry that his wife and sister-in-law were importing a tarnished Charleston belle to prove his adulterous inclinations.

The wronged wife was Shulteis's client, but the lawyer had political ambitions. Knowing whose side the bread was buttered on, and which gender has voting rights, Shulteis spared the man embarrassment and ensured his loyalty. A quiet, uncontested divorce was later obtained in another state.

Hiring me to secure evidence of LeBruton's alienated affections indicated that LeBruton's sphere of influence and personal wealth was negligible.

Abelia's hand delved her dress pocket. A money clip with quarter-folded banknotes materialized in her outstretched palm.

"I got nine dollars saved up that says you'll help me fix things so's Master LeBruton don't find out about Miz Penny showing him the door, before it's too late to stop his evil schemin'. There's more money—lots more—to come once the dust settles and Miz Penny is free of him."

"Oh, Abelia . . ." I dragged a stool over and sat down, suddenly too heartsick to stand. "Put your money away. Better yet, take it to the depot and buy Mrs. LeBruton a train ticket away from here. A divorce can't be granted in secret."

"Huh. Just 'cause I'm a nigger don't mean I'm igno-rant, missy. There's a heap of talking that goes on over the back fence. I'm telling you, if we're real careful, it can be done."

She crossed her arms at her chest. "First, do what you was hired for—prove that man is laying with other women." She snorted. "Shouldn't take more'n an hour."

"All right. Then what?"

"Tell Shulteis that Mr. Rendal's fixin' to spirit Miz Penny away and steal her money. Being a lawyer, he's li-able to know how to kibosh that notion. There's a fat fee in it for him, too, if he keeps his mouth shut and does a little sidewinding in our favor."

"But—"

"Will you hush up and *listen?*"

"Yes, ma'am."

"You can also tell him that I'll be seventy-three year old, come October, and I'd sooner hang for killing a lawyer as to die in my sleep."

I grinned. Devil take the agency's percentage. The look on Fulton's face when I delivered Abelia's message would be payment enough.

"What about the legal notice?" I asked. "Any suit filed with the court is public record and must be published in the newspaper."

"Nobody ever told me that." Scowling, Abelia tilted her

head to one side. "Are you for certain-sure? No insult meant, but the hem of your skirts ain't been let down to the ground for too many years."

"Oh, I'm certain, all right. Because Denver is the county seat, it must be published here."

Abelia clucked her tongue. "It'd be foolish to disbelieve you, but that's a sprag in the wagon wheel."

More like a sinkhole. Legend had it, a fire back in '63 and the Cherry Creek flood a year later almost wiped Denver City off the map, but neither stilled William Byers's printing press for long. Special editions of the *Rocky Mountain News* hit the streets within hours of those disasters.

"I'll pray on it real hard," Abelia said. "If faith can move a mountain, I reckon it can show us the road around one, too." The *bong* of the grandfather clock echoed from the foyer. Abelia gasped and tugged at my sleeve. "Lawsy mercy, if you're still here when that man gets home, our goose is cooked, girl."

She hustled me through the front kitchen and into the back. The sunny, whitewashed room was filled with racks of drying linens and unmentionables that smelled of soap and unslaked lime. Flat- and fluting irons of myriad sizes and weights rested on a tin-plated shelf above a small woodstove.

"Now don't you come back here again," Abelia said. "Miz Penny, she ain't allowed no company. Ain't allowed out of the house neither, unless Mr. Rendal's with her."

I started. "Then how did she make and keep an appointment with J. Fulton Shulteis?"

"The doctor treatin' Miz Penny for barrenness is two doors down and a floor up from the lawyer. That's 'bout the onliest place she can go without that man doggin' her heels."

My fist throttled my reticule's drawstring neck. Some people wouldn't recognize a blessing if it tapped a shoulder and said "Howdy-do." Babies aren't splints or breathing pots of bee balm. Bearing one to heal a fractured marriage was an abomination.

Abelia's palm at my back hastened my exodus out onto a planked stoop. "I shop every other morning 'tween nine and ten at Cheesman's Drug Store whilst His Nibs gets duded up to do nothing the livelong day."

The screen door patted shut against the jamb. "Meet me there come Thursday. I expect to hear something besides 'Good mornin', Abelia' when you do."

I was through the back gate and striding down the alleyway before I realized Abelia never had asked my name.

THREE

It is a fact of life that the greater hurry one is in to go somewhere, the less likely a means of transportation other than shoe leather will avail itself.

On the off-chance Fulton might still be in his office, I headed for Larimer Street as fast as my tired limbs would take me. Holding my reticule like a shield, I wove around hoards of lollygaggers with naught better to do than get in my way.

There ought to be a law.

Percy stepped out the door just as I rounded the corner. He fumbled with the key, his head bent, muttering at the lock as though inanimate objects must be cajoled to ensure cooperation. Papa had been a great one to speechify everything from wagon jacks to Rochester lamps, but his comments were colored the most exquisite shade of blue my ears had yet absorbed.

"Percy, thank goodness you're still here."

He whirled. Papers flew from his arms like snowbirds taking wing. Bowler askew, his spectacles hanging from one ear, he bellowed, "Now look what you've done."

"Me?" I knelt to scoop up the foolscap littering the boardwalk. "Ye gods, you're jumpier than froglegs in hot fat."

He righted his hat and eyeglasses, then squatted down beside me. "Please spare me the backwoods colloquialisms. I've heard quite enough of them for one day."

"I apologize, Percy. I truly didn't intend to startle you so fierce."

He stood. "Whatever your intentions, it's been an extremely trying day, and as you can see, I have reams of work ahead of me this evening."

"Then I won't bother you another second. I'll call on Mr. Shulteis tomorrow morning."

"He will be in court tomorrow and very probably the next."

The image of Penelope LeBruton, the wounded angel imprisoned in a gossamer cage, shimmered behind my eyes. It wasn't a matter of if her husband would make good his threat, but when. "One question is all I need ask, Percy. Surely he can find time for that."

He shrugged and started away. "The trial is in Leadville, Miss Sawyer. He left the city on the noon stage."

I assume my expression fell to the depths of woebegone, for Percy shifted his weight as though recalling his mother's instructions on gentlemanly behavior. In a tone as solemn as an undertaker's, he said, "Might I in some way be of assistance."

Eager as he was to please his employer, Percy was book smart, but he lacked the aptitude for creative thinking.

His type, I believed, was better suited for the accounting profession or government work.

In any event, I wasn't comfortable divulging the complications of the LeBruton case. Trustworthy or not, Percy hadn't read law long enough to familiarize himself with its intricacies, which afforded no help to me at all.

He could forward a letter to Fulton, but it would probably reach Leadville an hour after the attorney quit that city. What a telegram gained in speed, it sacrificed in discretion. Avoiding specifics would render my message unintelligible. "Now that I think about it," I said, "maybe you can be of assistance."

It was obviously not the hoped-for response, but I continued, "That is, if you'd loan me a book on territorial law pertaining to bills of divorcement." I tilted my head. "Unless you'd rather assist me in my research, it being on behalf of one of Fulton's clients and all." A dreamy sigh escaped my lips. "What a delightful evening that would be. Just the two of us. Alone. Together."

Blushing to the roots of his sandy hair, Percy could not fit the key in the office's door lock fast enough. He reexited a moment later with three leather-bound, gilt-embossed volumes, which he foisted into my waiting arms.

The books were as heavy as flagstones and pinched my corset's whalebone stays. Five long, sweltering blocks separated me from my Champa Street office—a fact of which Percy was undoubtedly aware and would celebrate with a cup of milky tea, his pinky finger raised in salute.

I simpered, "I can always count on you, Percy. Why, if I wasn't a lady, I swear, I'd kiss you smack on the lips."

He ducked behind a wall of papers. "Egads, woman. Restrain yourself!"

Two teamsters dodged around him, chuckling. One said, "Whoo-ee. If'n that pretty gal took a shine to me, danged if I'd fight her off."

Percy looked at them, then me, with equal disdain. "Well, I *never*."

The second man drawled, "We done figgered that already, son."

Before the law clerk dissolved to a puddle of embarrassment, I said, "Oh, mind your own business," to the men, then aimed a sweet smile at Percy. "Thank you very much for your help. The next time I see Fulton, I'll certainly put in a good word for you."

"As relating this incident would do nothing to further my career, I would prefer my employer remain ignorant of it."

Our eyes met. "Then it will be our little secret," I said. He knew I'd use it to finagle another favor someday. Such is the nature of commerce.

The ceaseless wind batted my hat and fed me sips of grit and soot as I made my way up Larimer. Or down it. Or specifically, in a due northeasterly direction, until I reached the corner of H, where I turned due south-southeast.

Had the city's founders possessed a thimbleful of horse sense—or sobriety—the folly of platting streets to intersect with the banks of Cherry Creek, rather than in accordance with a compass, might have occurred to them. As it had not, the entire metropolis was laid out antigoggling to the mountains, the sun, the moon—any and all topographic and celestial landmarks humankind has relied upon for navigation since the dawn of time.

Although Arkansas was graven on my soul and flavored my speech, Colorado in general and Denver City in particular had stolen my heart, as it had tens of thousands of gold-fevered come-heres who'd sallied west to make a fortune and found a home. I only wished the damnfool first arrivals had squared longitude with latitude like the rest of the world.

The smell of spilt beer and bodies several days removed from a bath wafted from every fifth or sixth doorway. Disembodied conversations and laughter chased out onto the street as well. Thankfully, it was too early in the evening for much gunplay.

Clattering away on a vacant lot between an auction-and-storage concern and a brothel were Aloysius Q. Dablemont and his steam-driven rainmaking machine. The balding, portly climatologist stood on a soapbox, his bowler aloft, telling the dozen or so folks gathered round that last night's mizzling rain was a mere sample of his contraption's wares. A pure-de-frog strangler was within his realm, but they cost extra and must be paid for in advance.

Further on, two mangy curs trotted behind an ice wagon, lapping at the water dripping under its doors. From the opposite direction came a dray heaped with offal. The dogs yelped and stutter-stepped. Their bone-sharp heads swiveled from one conveyance to the other.

The horns of their dilemma reminded me of my own. A legal means of snipping Mrs. LeBruton's bonds of unholy matrimony could be as close as a page in the godawful heavy books hugged to my bosom. If not, there was more up my leg-o'-mutton sleeve besides my arm.

It was resurrecting Papa for his appointment tomorrow with Misters McCoyne and Whitelaw that had me flummoxed. Men of their station and prestige would not be dissuaded by excuses, nor would they confide in Joe B.

Sawyer's able female assistant. Currying the carriage trade was vital to the agency's prosperity. The rent, expenses, and Sawyer Investigations' future could not be staked on crumbs tossed by J. Fulton Shulteis.

Before the appointed hour, what if I positioned Won Li behind a screen? Selling McCoyne and Whitelaw on the pretense that secrecy was crucial to covert investigations would take some fast, fancy talking. I'd emphasize the general knowledge that Wells, Fargo employed undercover operatives. So did the Pinkerton National Detective Agency. It stood to reason that stealth was a higher priority for a small concern like ours.

The hitch in that grand scheme was Won Li's adamant refusal to cooperate. Even if his faculties deserted him for a nonce and he agreed, the odds of him feigning a low-country Arkansas accent were equal to passing myself off as a deposed Hungarian princess.

I hated like sixty to admit it, but the only device left to me was the truth. That is, the shade of lavender that had come to simulate the truth for having told it to every Tom, Dick, and Harry who'd sought a personal audience with the agency's namesake.

The banker and the stamping mill owner would not be amused when informed that Papa's arrival in the city had been unavoidably delayed. Lo, it proximated gospel enough to pinch my soul whenever I thought it, much less said it aloud.

How ironic, being acclimated to him being abroad as much as he was home, my mind was still a storehouse of things tagged *Don't forget to tell Papa* and *Wait'll Papa hears this* or *sees that*. Bittersweet would be the day it became habit to take two plates from the cupboard instead of three.

Harp not on that string, I thought, quoting Shakespeare. Sagacious advice, and like most admonitions, a whole lot easier to say than heed.

A horse's familiar nicker reached my ears. Izzy, my father's Morgan gelding, was harnessed to our buggy, pulled up alongside the boardwalk. Having spent most of his life as a saddle-mount, his disdain at being relegated to part-time dray horse was pronounced.

No driver with a pigtail coiled under a gray felt Stetson occupied the buggy's seat. My heart tripped a beat. Seldom did Won Li wander afield. The neighborhood ran to seedy, and the Chinese were no better admired in Denver City than they were in Ft. Smith—or, to my knowledge, anywhere in the U.S. of A. It behooved him to wait with his chin tucked and hat brim pulled down like a bona fide, red-blooded American.

Why folks resented the Hop Alley denizens' cheap labor I couldn't comprehend, as few, if any, detractors would work as long and hard for the same coin.

Also a country mile short of endearing were the Occidentals' strange garb, singsong lingo, and peculiar customs. Conventional wisdom decreed that Chinese men lived in filth, feasted on rodents, gambled to excess, worshipped false idols, smoked opium, and lusted for white women. By contrast, Caucasians were pillars of hygiene, eschewed squirrels and beaver as entrees, were prudent gamblers and devout Christians whose lungs were as chaste as their fleshly desires. What mostly tied people's goat was the Asian proclivity for bowing, scraping, and all the while smiling like incumbent politicians. Won Li was an exception, but it seems that happy-go-luckiness can be construed as mockery and punished accordingly.

Fearing it had, my eyes fell on a tall, burly gent buttressing the agency's door frame. This time, it wasn't anxiety that put the skitter in my pulse. From our first meeting, city constable Jack O'Shaughnessy had sundry effects on my physiognomy. I wasn't prone to swoons, but that sly, mustachioed grin of his limbered my knees.

Jack was ten years my senior and a tick or two shy of handsome, as his features were hewn rugged by travail. He was of excellent character, however, and possessed of a ready humor.

The latter presented itself the night he and other members of the police force stormed Madame Felicity's sporting house. I was engaged in a high-kicking, petticoat-swirling cancan when Officer O'Shaughnessy swung me down from the bar to provide escort to a horse-drawn paddy wagon.

Into his ear, I'd whispered, "Please don't give me away, but I'm really not a dancer."

He'd grinned and drawled back, "Believe me, ma'am, I noticed that right off."

After J. Fulton Shulteis restored my good name, Jack began dropping by the office, claiming an eagerness to make Papa's acquaintance. When it became apparent I was the Sawyer in whom Jack was most interested, I informed him that romance was at the bottom on my list of ambitions.

"Happy to hear it," he'd said. "I'm not the marrying kind, either."

That took me aback, though by all rights, I should have been relieved. A woman of lesser gumption and greater arrogance might have felt insulted by his abrupt, categorical, unchivalrous, and seemingly intransigent immunity to her feminine wiles.

"Boon companions we'll be, then," I said. "Friendship without the onus of courtship."

"Yep. No entanglements, no expectations." He crooked a brow. "As long as one doesn't lead to the other."

"There's no reason to think it might, seeing as how we have this understanding between us."

"Uh-huh."

"And we aren't attracted to each other—well, not in *that* way. You know, how men and women usually are—giddy and breathless and wrought-up in each other's company."

Bent knuckles stroked my cheek, a caress all the more tender for his large, rough-skinned hands. "I can't speak for you," he'd drawled, "but as you can see, darlin', I'm not the least bit giddy or breathless."

Leaning into his touch, had I been a cat, I'd have purred. "Nor am I. Which is as it should be, between . . . er, friends."

"Ummhmm." He licked his lips, hovering inches from mine, but as I stretched upward on tiptoes, he'd pulled back. "I wouldn't want you any other way."

It was then I knew that lying with a straight face was but one of many things Jack O'Shaughnessy and I had in common.

Friendship swelled inside me as I traversed the few remaining steps to the agency's entrance. Jack grinned and doffed his narrow-brimmed hat. Rather than his dark wool, brass-buttoned uniform, he was dressed in striped trousers, a black frock coat, starched white shirt, and a string tie. A lilt of bay rum sweetened the air.

"Nothing dire has befallen Won Li, has it?" I asked.

Jack lifted the law books from my arms. He gave their

titles a cursory examination, then turned his sky blue eyes on me. "When I left him, he was strawbossing the youngsters he hired to rebuild the toolshed. Again."

A blush crawled warm up my neck. "The slightest breeze would have blown it over."

"Might could," he allowed, "but blowing it to hell and gone took a crazy woman and a beaker of nitrostarch."

"I am *not* crazy. I'm a scientist."

Jack rested a hand on my shoulder. "We've already plowed this ground, darlin'. It scares the liver out of me that someday you'll end up six feet under it."

"Oh, and constables are renowned for longevity?"

He didn't reply. Not because a half-dozen of them weren't rattling round inside that thick skull of his. Unlike Papa, Jack knew instinctively that bellowing and blustering stiffened my backbone, whereas silence allowed guilt an opportunity to nibble at my conscience.

I delved into my reticule for the door key. Blasting through the shed's roof had dislodged all memory of Jack's invitation to supper and a minstrel show. Then again, the LeBruton business had been uppermost in my mind, seconded by the McCoyne/Whitelaw conundrum, plus the sorry state of the agency's finances.

As I strode into the furnace the office had become in my absence, I considered excusing myself from the evening's plans. Duty had called Jack away several times in the past, with no remonstrations from me.

However, Dr. Thaddeus MacKenzie, a Boston psychologist of regard, hypothesized that interludes of mental leisure invigorated the brain, just as napping did the body. What better time than the present to test the veracity of his theory?

An hour later, Jack and I were seated in the Tremont

House's dining room, tucking into platters of beefsteak and the customary trimmings. The wine he'd ordered to accompany the meal shone like liquid rubies contained in a crystal goblet. I'd read that a taste for wine was an acquired one, but never guessed an affection for such a tart, dry beverage could develop between the first, puckery sips and the second glassful.

Jack's fork paused between the plate and his mouth. "So, you were summoned to Shulteis's office again, eh?" He angled his head. "Before you curse Won Li for tattletaling, the endleaves of those books you were toting had J. Fulton Shyster's seal embossed on them."

For reasons unknown, I couldn't muster a jot of irritation. Cops are as inquisitive as private investigators—and their daughterly assistants, as it were. My tone was teasing when I said, "You're quite the nosy Parker, aren't you, Constable?"

"No more than you, Miz Sawyer."

I dabbed my lips with a linen napkin. The Tremont House didn't skimp on the amenities. Their week's laundry bill would put me in tall cotton for the balance of the year. "Are you familiar with a man by the name of Rendal LeBruton?"

Jack chewed and swallowed a chunk of pan-broiled potato before answering. "I'm proud of you, Joby. We almost got a whole meal down before the interrogation commenced."

"A simple question does not an interrogation make."

"That's true. It's just the warning shot." To onlookers, his expression suggested an unconsummated belch.

I wasn't fooled for a second. Crime and criminals were his cerebral meat and potatoes. For all intents, Jack's rank was municipal detective. The official promotion and pay raise were stalemated until the city approved a departmental funding increase.

"Rendal LeBruton, eh?" he said. "On the runty side? Brown hair and a Vandyke beard?"

I nodded. The description jibed with a framed tintype I'd seen on Penelope's lowboy chest of drawers. Papa always said folks are leery of big men and large dogs, but it's the small end of both species that bears watching.

Jack leaned on his forearms and lowered his voice. "I know you won't betray a confidence, but if Shulteis hired your father to get the goods on Mrs. LeBruton, I'd take care not to let her hear it on the wind."

"Oh?" I struggled for nonchalance. "Far be it for me to argue, but Joe B. Sawyer can hold his own against any mere slip of a female." I smiled. "Present company excluded."

"It's apples to oranges, darlin'. You're as whip-smart, adventurous, and ornery as any gal in the Territories, but there isn't a mean bone in your body. On the other hand, I hear the LeBruton woman is a hellion when she's drunk and she's seldom, if ever, sober."

The child-sized blonde's transmutation to a sozzled Medusa didn't quite parse. "Heard from whom?"

Speaking a mite softer than the scrape of utensils on china and orbital conversations, Jack said, "About a month ago, we got a report of a ruckus at the LeBruton house. The beat cops found an ungodly mess—broken bric-a-brac, furniture upturned, and the wife in a heap at the bottom of the stairs. Mr. LeBruton said the missus lunged at him with a butcher knife. Missed him by a yard, but she lost her balance and tumbled down the stairs, knife in hand. Pure luck she didn't break her fool neck. LeBruton begged the constables to keep mum about the whole affair."

Disgust soured my stomach. Under my breath, I murmured, "I'll just bet he did."

"Beg pardon?"

I waved a dismissal. "You said someone reported the fight. Who, exactly?"

"I don't know, *exactly*." Jack's chuckle was indulgent. "Probably a neighbor, or a passerby. It wasn't the first call the police have paid there. Won't be the last, either, I'll warrant."

A crease pinched between my brows. My audience with Penelope LeBruton was of less than five minutes' duration. I'd assumed Rendal to be the aggressor the moment I saw her.

Abelia loathed him, but taking her word that he was a wife-beating swindler was akin to Rendal coaching the police into believing Penelope was a harridan and a drunkard.

Bullpats. I'd smelled not a whiff of strong spirits in the house, nor any perfumed artifice to mask the scent. If Penelope was a dipsomaniac, she accomplished it without the telltale puffiness about the eyes, a hint of tremor in her hands, or blooms at her cheeks and nose caused by dilated capillaries.

Asking Jack if the alleged butcher knife was found at the scene was as moot as defending the accused. His information was secondhand, whereas my contention was intuitive, although I'd be fascinated to hear how anyone, drunk or sober, could hurtle down a flight of stairs clutching a large knife without slicing or stabbing oneself to a fare-thee-well. Had Penelope done so, the station house rumors and Jack's repetition of them would have included a grisly account of her injuries.

The logical conclusion was that Rendal LeBruton's

campaign to asperse his wealthy wife and portray himself as a loving, helpless husband was well under way.

There would be a lamp burning late into the night at the clapboard cottage Won Li and I shared. If God was merciful, the books I borrowed would supply a loophole to allow compliance with the law in regard to printed notices, while lessening the odds of the respondent learning of it.

Except loopholes had the frequent and nasty habit of becoming nooses. I dashed such thoughts with a healthy swallow of wine.

FOUR

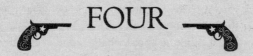

The night was star-bright and deliciously cool when Jack and I emerged from the Denver Theatre onto Lawrence Street. The minstrel show, a troupe late of Cheyenne and bound for Salt Lake City, had me in stitches one minute and dew-eyed the next when a tenor keened "The Maid of Monterey."

Jack's arm captured my waist to negotiate the throng disbursing to the line of waiting phaetons, wagonettes, buckboards, and buggies. My elbow bumped the holstered revolver concealed by his coat. The badge authorizing its service was pinned to an inside lapel.

Little did he know, his lady friend carried more than a clean hanky and female possibles in her reticule. Although not as readily accessible, a sweet, pearl-handled derringer rested within the drawstring ties, along with spare cartridges, bottled smoke powders, a tin of flash powder, tincture of Morpheus, smelling salts, and a string of tiny Chinese firecrackers.

Like private investigators, constables were never completely off-duty and supplied their own weapons, but they were dunned the cost of their uniforms and earned a salary equal to a greenhorn cowhand. Just as when Papa was a U.S. marshal, I wondered why men of such intelligence and grit chose to be peace officers.

Jack gave my ribs a squeeze. "You know what they say. Beware the quiet woman and rattlesnakes."

"I was just thinking about what a wonderful time I had this evening." I winked up at him. "Dinner and the show were nice, too."

He laughed—a great booming sound, like barrels rolling off a wagon. "Then I reckon we should step out more often."

"Do you know what I'd truly love to do someday?" I took his hand for a boost into the buggy.

Tease that he was, Jack wiggled his eyebrows. "Marry an Irishman and have six sons and two daughters all named for the patron saints?"

Our gazes locked, each daring the other to blink. "Eight children? Are you insane?"

"Four, then."

"Two. A boy and a girl." I patted my hair, as women do when thoroughly discombobulated. "But first, I want to take a horseback ride. Law, it's been a coon's age since Izzy's had a fast, cross-country gallop. Or me, for that matter."

The Morgan's ears swiveled. He stamped a forehoof, as though casting his vote in favor.

Grinning huge, Jack started around the buggy.

"We could pack a lunch," I babbled on. "Make a day of it. After the heat relents, of course. Early fall would be nice. When the leaves are turning."

"Sounds good to me." He took the seat beside me and unwrapped the reins from the whip-socket. A tongue cluck eased the buggy forward as smooth as a sleigh on ice. "Maybe earlier than that. I'll have more free time when the men the chief loaned out to Sheriff Kite for posse duty get back."

A rash of Indian raids had impelled the newspaper to admonish, "Fear of Indians should not discourage rail travel in Colorado. Both the Denver and Kansas Pacifics are well guarded and the redmen know it."

The police chief's contribution to public safety had been to assign a squadron of constables to help capture the renegades. The department was already undermanned, but railroads were the lifeblood of progress and prosperity.

"No rush," I said. "I have business aplenty to attend myself."

"Which includes introducing me to your father, before we head for the hills alone together." Jack's sidelong glance was brief but no-nonsense. "Darlin', it'd be tragic on a grand scale if that look on your face got stuck, permanent."

"Don't you darlin' me, Jack O'Shaughnessy. I'm a grown woman and perfectly capable of—"

"Respecting her elders' respect for her."

As we turned onto G Street, I crossed my arms tight at my chest, bereft of a reply. God save the fairer sex from old-fashioned notions—especially those Papa would endorse.

I trusted Jack second only to Won Li, but his provincial attitude sealed my lips against confiding the secret of Joseph Beckworth Sawyer's demise. No one but Izzy knew of my dreams to create the world's first all-female detective agency, specializing in the curtailment of stagecoach and train robberies. What gang of thieves would ever suspect lady passengers to let fly with sulphuric smoke bombs and disarm them while their eyes stung and wept from the fumes?

Quite the lofty ambition for one who must have her father's permission to venture beyond the city limits with her boon companion and a picnic basket.

The buggy lurched as Izzy shied from three jaywalkers. Their entwined arms united them against Taos Lightning's "strikes hard and leaves nothing standing" reputation. The Mexican firewater was said to be laced with gunpowder and strained through kegs of rusty nails to dissolve impurities such as thirsty insects, snakes, and small woodland critters.

The drunk pedestrians tottered backward as one. The biggest lout bellowed, " 'Ey, watch where you're goin', bub."

Before Jack could respond, a horse came a whisker from colliding with us on the driver's side. The rider swiveled around in the saddle, looked back, then reined in his mount, as if a wall had risen phoenix-like in front of him.

"O'Shaughnessy! Praise glory, is that you?"

Jack squinted through the billowing dust. "Hopkins? Holy Moses, man. Where's the fire?"

"A murder's been done. Colonel Abercrombie's, on California Street. Follow me."

"But—" Jack looked at me. His expression was as legible as ten-point type. Requisition the buggy and leave me afoot? Hand me the reins and sprint after Hopkins? Haste me home? Or take me along?

Nails digging my palms, I sincerely believed I'd scream before he faced forward and shouted, "Hi-*yah*."

The reins snapped smart on the Morgan's rump. Pell-mell, we raced after Constable Hopkins. Izzy's shod hooves tattooed the packed earth. The rig swayed, its wheels jouncing over ruts sliced by heavier, broader conveyances.

We slowed not at all at intersections. I imagined oncoming ore-wagons and fatal consequences but decided not to inquire why a deceased person was in need of such breakneck attendance.

I knew Colonel Abercrombie's title was honorary, in the tradition of Southern women being referred to as Miss, whether young, aged, married, or confirmed spinsters.

Abercrombie owned several department stores scattered throughout the Territory. Via his original mercantile in Kansas City, he'd grubstaked Colorado-bound prospectors in exchange for shares in their as-yet undug mines and creekside claims. Enough of them reaped such handsome rewards that Abercrombie had sold his Missouri store and reestablished himself in Denver City.

Constable Hopkins's arm signaled a turn to the left ahead. The buggy careered on two wheels around the corner and would have evicted me had I not braced my feet on the floorboard and throttled the armrest.

My impressions of California Street were swift-drawn. It was more residential than commercial, but vacant lots outnumbered those developed for either usage. Transplanted cottonwoods, elms, and maples lined its parkway and would eventually shade the earthen street.

At midblock, a pinkish sandstone mansion was ablaze with light. Every mullioned window, of which there were multitudes, vanquished the darkness. An amber flood streamed out of the open, double-doored entrance.

Rubberneckers gathered on the manicured lawn, unmindful of flower beds, shrubbery, and common decency. One enterprising lad had climbed onto the fountain, affording himself a ringside perch and a bath in the massive, scalloped bowl.

Jack halted the buggy in the crushed stone driveway. He stepped out, holding the reins for my slide across the seat. "I hate leaving you to drive yourself home."

"It can't be helped. Don't worry, I'll be fine."

He kissed my cheek and smiled, though I could see his mind was already fixed on what horrors might be found inside the house. "Straight home, Joby. And keep your eyes peeled for ruffians."

I promised I would. I didn't promise when that journey might commence. Before Jack's broad back disappeared into the mansion's glowing maw, I took a small notebook and pencil from my reticule, then cached the bag under the seat.

Izzy's black coat shone with lather from his southward lope. Poor fella was blowing some, too. I patted his mane and told him his pluck and patience would later be rewarded with an apple and a bucket of oats.

Just inside the Abercrombies' foyer, an urn of Grecian design full of hothouse flowers had been toppled from its table onto the white marble floor. On a bench curved to conform with the muraled wall, a Negro manservant comforted a maid sobbing into a dishtowel. Both were dressed in nightclothes.

The manservant glanced up. His red-rimmed eyes narrowed with suspicion.

"I'm Josephine Sawyer, of Sawyer Investigations." I displayed my notebook. "There are questions I must ask of you momentarily, but do take this respite to compose yourselves."

He nodded, returning his attention to the maid, now hiccoughing with every breath.

A relieved sigh blew through my lips. Acting with authority was often as good as having some. The Denver City police force employed no women, but my dark blue suit was as tailored as a uniform and had small brass buttons at the placket and cuffs.

My gaze tracked the elegant, serpentine stairway from where disembodied voices drifted downward. Turning, I surveyed the distance from the top of the stairs to the mahogany front doors. Heavy brass locks, as sturdy as they were decorative, gleamed against the ruddy wood.

A plush runner of tapestried wool protected the stairway's treads and muffled the footfalls of anyone trafficking upon them—most certainly, mine. The voices guided me down a wide corridor painted a rich egg cream color and trimmed in purest white.

At its end, in a soft-lit room, a girl of perhaps eighteen sat in a wing chair drawn up beside a bed. Wisps of hair had escaped their pins and veiled her features. She was murmuring to a gray-haired man lying beneath a shawl, a hand tented over his face. A Bible marked with a scarlet ribbon lay open on the end of the bed.

Colonel Abercrombie, I presumed, and his daughter. Her name I'd read in the newspaper's society page, but couldn't recall. Thinking of all the bedside vigils I'd sat with Papa when he'd come home sick, or hurt, or nigh delirious from exhaustion, a stab of envy startled, then shamed me. Just because my father was lost to me in this life, it was horrid to begrudge Miss Abercrombie hers.

An open door on my left revealed a boudoir decorated in blush pinks, golds, and ivory. Jack knelt beside the figure of a woman clad in an aqua dressing gown. She was sprawled on her back in a most indelicate position. Her hair was long, wavy, and the color of chestnuts. I guessed her to be in her early thirties.

What had been a fair complexion was splotchy and mottled. A double strand of pearls was cinched round her slender throat. Blood-tinged welts ribbed the skin above and below. Her eyes were closed as though in sleep, but her expression of sheer terror she'd take to the grave.

Two men stood near her slippered feet, their hands clasped in front of them. One was Constable Hopkins. The other was unknown to me. I slipped behind them into the chamber, hoping for a few seconds' reconnoiter before anyone took notice.

Two massive, claw-footed wardrobes stood like sentries in the corners of the room's far end. The doors were closed and locked with tassled keys. Between them was an upholstered settee strewn with a rather ugly saffron dress, a chemise, petticoats, and stockings. A silver coffee service rested on a tray table in front of it.

Pricey gilded statuettes, receptacles, candlesticks, and foofaraws were displayed on matching, marble-topped dressers and chests. Separately, the accessories were pieces of art. In toto, each was as distinctive as a pile of autumn leaves.

The carved walnut bed whose headboard rose within an inch of the ceiling had been neatly turned down, but the bottom sheet was rumpled and a pillow was askew and devoid of its lace-trimmed casing. Nearby was a mirrored dressing table cluttered with crystal atomizers, pots of creams and lotions, a monogrammed silver brush, hand mirror and comb, and ornate trinket boxes. The lower drawers had been rifled; the contents of the two deeper ones were dumped on the floor.

A draft wended from French doors accessing onto a balcony. I moved nearer, stepping carefully over a jewelry case laying splayed open and empty on the Brussels carpet. I'd just glimpsed a rope knotted around one of the balcony's wrought-iron rails when a hand gripped my arm and none too gently.

"Judas priest." Jack glowered down at me, a spark of homicidal mania in his eye. Through clenched teeth, he said, "What the *hell* are you doing up here?"

"Investigating."

"Snooping's more like it."

"It appears the victim interrupted another burglary-in-progress and paid with her life. I don't recollect the newspaper mentioning the rope was left behind at the McCoyne and Whitelaw robberies, but the uncased pillow—"

"Joby—"

I grimaced and tried pulling from his grasp. "You're hurting me." He wasn't, but he apologized and unhanded me all the same.

My eyes slid to the dead woman. Constable Hopkins had removed his coat and laid it over her head and torso. "If that's Mrs. Abercrombie, she's not much older than her daughter."

"Stepdaughter. The deceased, first name Belinda, is— was—Hubert Abercrombie's second wife."

"Oh? How long have they been married?"

"I don't know yet, and it's none of your concern." Jack looked over his shoulder at the other men. "Now you scat back to that buggy and hie for home."

"No."

He started. "*No?*"

"You can force my ejection, if you care to make a scene." I jutted my chin. "A screaming, shin-kicking donnybrook, similar to our encounter at Madame Felicity's."

His voice dropped an octave. "Are you threatening me, Miz Sawyer?"

Of course I was, but only figuratively. If Jack called my bluff, I'd exit with all respect due the departed and her loved ones. "Oh, don't be such a fusspot. Just ignore me altogether. You know I won't meddle in your investigation."

"You already have."

"Observing is not meddling and this matter does concern me. This very afternoon, Garret McCoyne and Avery Whitelaw showed keen interest in hiring my father to recover the jewels stolen in the prior robberies."

Jack shifted his weight, as if debating whether to assist me bodily out the front door, or perhaps the balcony, versus a more sedate approach to my unofficial presence. "Lord have mercy, if the chief ever finds out . . ."

"Well, I certainly won't tell him, and I'm sure your men can be persuaded against carrying tales."

He massaged his brow, muttering a psalm. The Twenty-third, I believe. "All right, but make yourself scarce before the coroner gets here. He's had it in for me ever since he declared that ax murder last February a suicide."

I tendered a demure nod to Hopkins and the other man, then decamped. As I traversed the corridor, I recorded in my notebook the burglar's method of egress, a description of the pillow slip, and the relative positions of the French doors, jewel case, and the body.

I'd have preferred interviewing the household staff downstairs, but would delay until the coroner was sequestered in Belinda Abercrombie's bedroom.

Her husband and stepdaughter were still lodged in the room at the end of the hall. She seemed bewildered by my introduction but said her name was Avilla and confirmed her relationship to the deceased.

Hubert Abercrombie invited me to take a second wing chair. He was in his fifties, but his skin was as yellowish as tallow.

"I'm so sorry for your loss, Mr. Abercrombie."

"Did you know Belinda?" he asked.

"Miss Sawyer is with the police, Father."

I saw no reason to correct Avilla on a minor technicality.

Mr. Abercrombie beseeched the patterned ceiling. "Avilla and I were right here when—" Pain suffused his expression. "How could this have happened? And why?"

Avilla sighed and sat back in her chair. "It wouldn't have had we dined with the Estabrooks as planned."

I noted the name and question-marked it. At the time of the previous burglaries, the owners had been away for the evening.

Avilla went on to explain that Belinda had complained of an upset stomach shortly after lunch. "When it didn't abate, I sent Jules to the Estabrooks with a note of apology."

"Jules is your butler?"

"Majordomo, actually. He's been with Father for as long as I can remember." Anticipating my next question, Avilla added, "Jules's wife, Pansy, is our maid, and we have a cook—Gertrude Hiss. She's only been on staff a few months."

"Did your former cook resign?"

"Retired. Yolonda was almost a second mother to me—or grandmother, I suppose. She moved with us from Kansas City, but instead of helping, the mountain air only worsened her rheumatism."

Avilla frowned. "I'm not terribly fond of Gertrude's cooking, but my stepmother's people were a generation's remove from the Old Country. For Belinda, I think the sauerbraten and gurkensalat were like letters from home."

I asked, "Were Mrs. Abercrombie and Gertrude acquainted before she was hired to cook for you?"

"Of a sort. Gertrude's mother and Belinda's father were distant cousins." Avilla hastened to add, "So distant, Gertrude and Belinda weren't aware of the relation until they stumbled upon it in conversation, after Gertrude was hired."

"It must have been odd, learning that an employee was kin."

"Four or five times removed," Avilla stressed. "Hardly more than a coincidence, really. Gertrude was glad to have the work. If Belinda played favorites with the staff, I never saw it."

Ah, but had Gertrude expected her to?

A moan rattled out from Mr. Abercrombie's throat. "How'll we ever break the news to Belinda's poor mother? She's still in mourning for her husband, and now—"

"Just rest, Father. I'll see to it. I'll see to everything."

"*Murdered.* Almighty God, what is this world coming to?"

New male voices and a terrible racket funneled down the corridor. The coroner, who was also an undertaker, had arrived with his lackeys. Any who spied me would take me for a neighbor or family friend, but it wouldn't be long before inquiries of an official nature were launched.

"Mr. Abercrombie, can you tell me how the evening transpired after Jules was dispatched to the Estabrooks?"

Avilla shot me a scathing look. I understood her desire to spare her father more anguish, but such was impossible in a homicide investigation.

Abercrombie waved an arm as though swatting at a

moth. "We ate a cold supper, then my wife retired to her bedchamber to rest. The next I knew, Pansy screamed and burst in here, shouting that Belinda was dead."

Avilla patted, then chafed, his hand. Her fingers were as long and tapered as a pianist's, but every nail was bitten to the quick. "Father and I reviewed store accounts after supper. We partook of a brandy in the library, then came up here, as is our custom. He isn't much of a reader, but enjoys listening to Bible passages."

She smiled. "When I was little, reading wasn't my best subject in school. Our nightly ritual began as recitations. Now Father teases me about spending too much time with my nose in a book."

Papa had done the same, only his tone was thankful, not teasing. Until curiosity propelled me toward physics, pyrotechnics and chemistry, as long as I had a book in hand, I wasn't wreaking havoc on the citizens of Ft. Smith.

"Did either of you see Mrs. Abercrombie when you came upstairs?"

"She was fine—still queasy, but her stomach was settling when I checked on her," Mr. Abercrombie said. "I kissed her. Told her I'd peek in again before retiring for the night."

"How long was that before Pansy raised the alarm?"

"An hour," Avilla said. "A few minutes beyond, at most."

My eyes flicked to the mantel clock. It wasn't ticking, and the hands were stopped at twenty-five past three.

"Father had decided to sleep here, in the guest room, tonight. He hasn't left it since we came upstairs to read."

Abercrombie's head rose from the pillow. "I should have stayed with Belinda. If I had, she'd . . ." He sank back again. "My fault. It's all my fault, she's gone from us."

Avilla smoothed the hair from his brow. "Hush, now. That's just grief talking. How could you—how could anyone have known she was in danger?"

"She was ill. I shouldn't have left her alone."

Avilla looked at me, tears rising in her eyes. "I don't mean to be rude, Miss Sawyer, but I must ask you to go. My father and I have had a horrible shock, and his health is far from good."

"Of course." I repeated my condolence, then paused at the doorway. "One last thing, Mr. Abercrombie. I couldn't help but notice the bruise on your left hand. I'd be happy to fetch a cold cloth, to keep down the swelling."

He blinked at the darkening contusion equidistant from the base of his thumb and index finger. Avilla caught his hand in hers and lowered both to the bed. "That's very kind of you, but Father has suffered from anemia since he was a boy. When his blood is thin, a fly lighting on him would leave footprints."

Nodding, I turned away and started down the corridor. Was Avilla's protectiveness of her father understandable, or diversionary? A bit of both, I decided, giving quarter to the circumstances. She had, after all, answered my questions in a straightforward manner. Had I been in her place, I'd have likely put aside my sorrow and taken charge of the situation, too.

My relief at seeing the closed door to Belinda Abercrombie's room was momentary. While the coroner would remain ignorant of my presence, the thick, four-paneled oak door denied any possibility of eavesdropping on the conversation within.

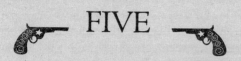

FIVE

"I'm Glover Rudd," said the perspiring young man at the foot of the staircase. His checked suit was frayed at the lapels and cuffs, and his shirt collar ringed his neck like a barrel stave around a fence pole. "Who are you and what can you tell me about the robbery/murder?"

I brushed past him.

"Madame, please. I'm a reporter for the *Rocky Mountain News*. The public has a right to know the facts surrounding this tragedy."

Greed slowed my stride. Attaching Sawyer Investigations to a crime of this magnitude could rate more attention than a paid advertisement. Then, as if Confucius—in the guise of Won Li—were astraddle my shoulder, I heard him say, *Cultivated people seek from themselves; small people seek from others.*

At times such as these, I sincerely wished I'd devoted more study to the culinary arts than philosophy. Without a word to Mr. Rudd, the aroma of brewing coffee guided me to the kitchen.

Pansy and Jules were making finger sandwiches for the constabulary and associated officials. I declined to partake of them but gratefully accepted a cup of strong, black coffee. I'd never tasted better, nor needed a stimulant more.

To Pansy, I said, "Busy hands occupy the mind, but I don't think I'd have your strength of will."

She chuffed. A sidelong glance affirmed my sincerity. Her expression registered surprise. Quietly, she said, "I'll see Miss Belinda, layin' there onna floor likes a broken doll, in my sleep till the day I die."

"What drew you to her room, Pansy? Or were you just securing the house for the night?"

"Me an' Jules were already abed." She hastened to add, "Mister Abercrombie tol' us nothin' needed doin' the rest of the evenin'. Heard a terrible crash, I did. I laid there a minute, listenin' real hard. Wasn't sure if 'twas a dream that woke me."

"That's when she roused me, for a look-see," Jules said.

"Huh. Wasn't like you jumped up and went a-runnin', ol' man." Pansy filleted the seeds from a cucumber. "Snorin' loud as thunder, he was. Bein' nigh deaf in his good ear, I had to thunk him a lick or three, 'fore he paid me any mind."

Jules grunted and moved to pour coffee from an urn into a serving carafe. "The front doors was standin' wide open. It a-frighted me—that pretty vase in shards on the floor and flowers strewed ever' which-a-way."

"Poor man, thought he'd forgot to lock up and the wind had shoved that jardiniere clean off'n the table." Pansy pointed the knife tip at her bosom. "Me, I knew in my heart it wasn't no wind that done it. Whilst Jules went about the downstairs rooms, I took myself upstairs.

" 'Twas peaceful as a churchhouse on a Tuesday, up yonder. I was near onto believin' it *was* the wind, but reckoned I'd best tell Miss Belinda 'bout the mess, or the master, if she was sleepin'."

Her voice faltered. Head bowed, she braced her fists against the worktable. Fat tears meandered from the corners of her eyes. Jules gave me an angry look as he wrapped an arm about his wife's trembling shoulders.

As gently as I could, I said, "I know how it must hurt to talk about what happened, but Mrs. Abercrombie can no longer speak for herself. If her killer is to be found, everything you saw and heard is of utmost importance."

"My wife already tol' you, ma'am," Jules said. "Whoever done it was long gone before we got out'n our bed."

Pansy shrugged off his arm. "See to the cups and saucers, ol' man. Napkins, too. The lady's only tryin' to help Miss Belinda."

Grumbling under his breath, Jules stalked off to the back kitchen.

"He's as heartbroke as I am," she said, "but mens, they don't let their feelin's show. Worse for it, too, if you ask me."

I thought of Papa, Jack O'Shaughnessy, and, most especially, Won Li. "They're raised to believe it's a sign of weakness."

Pansy nodded. "They're raised to believe a lot of things that's wrongheaded and twists their innards inside out. Maybe that's how the Lord intended, them being created in His image and all, but even a grizzly bear lets out a howl when a thorn's stuck in its paw."

I smiled at the reminder that wisdom wasn't unique to Confucius. Taking up a table knife to spread butter on the bread she'd sliced, I said, "I was under the impression that Gertrude Hiss was a live-in cook."

"She is." Pansy glared in the direction of the servant's quarters at the back of the house. "Mind you, I'm not one to carry tales, but this ain't the first time Gert's snuck out of an evenin' to meet up with Sam Merck. He's the gardener by day and plays faro, most nights. From what I've seen, Sam's no better at cards than he is with a rake and shovel."

Even when faro was dealt fair and square, and it rarely was at Denver City's gambling hells, "bucking the tiger" was a fool's game with the odds stacked well in favor of the house.

The layout consisted of a beaded rack, similar to an abacus. Beneath the strung beads were painted reproductions of the nine numeric four face cards, and ace in a standard deck. The pattern was duplicated on a boxlike frame.

The beads tracked the cards played, regardless of suit, revealed by the dealer's every two-card draw. Wagers were placed on what card would be turned next, or against a card's appearance. Simple as it sounded, few left the game with their pockets weighted with coins.

Pansy said, "Gert's later comin' home tonight than usual. If Miss Avilla or Mister Abercrombie ask after her, I won't give her up, but I won't lie for her, neither."

"What time did she leave?"

"I don't rightly know. Before supper is as near as I can say. The family was s'posed to eat with the Estabrooks this evenin'."

Meaning the cook wasn't aware those plans were cancelled at the last minute. Could she be the burglar's accomplice? Reminding myself that gender shouldn't exclude half the population from suspicion, Gertrude Hiss could be a cook by day and a thief by night.

"Does Sam Merck work here every day?" I asked.

"Not on the Sabbath." Pansy began arranging the finished sandwiches on a doily-covered tray. "As if Sam's prone to bend a knee, 'lessen he spies a nickel shining in the street."

"If someone wasn't acquainted with Sam Merck and Gertrude Hiss, how would you describe them?"

As I'd hoped, the answer painted disparaging portraits. Ask a person to describe a close friend, and physical flaws and abnormalities will be minimized, if mentioned at all. The less a person admires another, the more accurate the verbal picture—minus strokes of exaggeration.

Gertrude Hiss's hair was stringy, short-cropped as a boy's, and tinted a bright henna. Of average height and sturdy build, she had a bulbous nose, weak chin, and a raspy voice due to the corncob pipe she smoked behind a mulberry tree when she thought no one was looking.

As for Sam Merck, he was barrel-chested, broad-shouldered, and had dishwater blonde hair combed back from a widow's peak—when it wasn't hanging in his narrow-set eyes. Snaggle-toothed and hame-jawed, he wasn't exactly ugly, but Pansy said if she didn't know Sam, she'd hold her purse tighter to her chest if she passed him on the street.

"I keep it hid in my room as it is," she added. "Jules pokes fun at me for it, but I don't trust a man that throws hard-earned money away at a card table."

"Do the Abercrombies trust Sam Merck?" I asked.

"All he does is keep the grounds, miss. He ain't allowed inside the house."

I waggled my head in confusion. "Then why do you hide your purse from him?"

"That's perzackly what Jules says." Pansy sighed as though both of us were daft. "Just 'cause Sam ain't supposed to come in, don't mean he won't ever."

Some of us perceived *can't*, *won't*, and *don't* as dares. In my youth, if Papa hadn't been so enamored of all three, whippings might have been fewer and further between.

I flipped back to the page with Sam's and Gertrude's descriptions. I'd seen them somewhere. At the restaurant? The minstrel show? Oh, well. The sooner I stopped thinking about it, the sooner I'd remember.

"After Jules found the front doors open, was Avilla reading to her father when you went upstairs?"

"Yes, ma'am."

"You saw them."

"Yes'm." Pansy took a cucumber from the stack and munched it, absently. "Well, now I think on it, the door was shut, just like Miss Belinda's. They was there, though. After I saw Miss Belinda had gone to Jesus, I ran down the hall and pounded on the door, screamin' for help.

"Miss Avilla rushed out, and Mr. Abercrombie, fast as he's able. Jules came, too, then he went back downstairs. He hailed a buggy passin' by and tol' 'em a murder had been done and to go for the police."

Crockery tinked together as Jules reentered the kitchen. "Shows how good you remember. The master stumbled and near fainted away when he saw Miss Belinda like that. Me and Miss Avilla took him back down the hall, 'fore he tol' me to fetch the po-lice."

"The police," I repeated. "Not a doctor."

Jules removed a stack of ironed napkins from a drawer.

"If he'd asked for a doctor, that's what I'd have sent those people to fetch."

"Did he check Mrs. Abercrombie's pulse? Put a mirror under her nose? Did anyone?"

Jules's and Pansy's eyes met. Her hand went to her mouth. "Oh, no. We didn't, did we? I never . . . Oh, my Lord."

"No need for it," he snapped back, "and I'll thank you kindly not to upset my wife. Miss Belinda was dead where she laid. I can promise you that."

I sipped my coffee and entered a few notes to allow the tension to subside. Pansy was sniffling again. I was sorry for the doubt I'd planted, but the question wasn't mean-spirited or frivolous.

I listed the four people who'd entered the room at least once: Pansy, Avilla, Hubert Abercrombie, and Jules. In that instance, a physician would be remiss to declare death by sight alone. Besides, wasn't it instinctive to check for life-signs?

Could the shock of seeing his wife strangled with a string of her own pearls have unhinged Hubert Abercrombie that badly? Possibly, yet moments later, he had the presence of mind to send his manservant for help.

A thought stilled my hand. What if Abercrombie didn't check his wife's pulse or respiration because he knew she was dead before he entered the room? Knew even before Pansy screamed? That would explain those lapses and why the authorities were summoned instead of a doctor.

But not the burglary, dash it all.

Without cognizance of it, Rendal LeBruton's cruelty to his wife must be influencing my deductions in this case. And how tidy it would be to wangle the earlier robberies into decoys, albeit lucrative ones, for a LeBruton/Abercrombie conspiracy. Rendal murdered Belinda, Hubert will return the favor by killing Penelope a few days hence, thus each has disposed of a problematic wife and ensured himself against the other's betrayal or blackmail.

"You got any more questions, miss?" Pansy startled me from plotting what might be the perfect double-homicide.

"Just a few," I stammered. "What did you do after Avilla and Mr. Abercrombie returned to the guest room and Jules went downstairs?"

"Sat myself down on the steps and bawled." Pansy swiped the back of a hand under her eyes. "That's what."

"Do you know where Sam Merck lives?"

"Not perzackly."

Pansy's demeanor had taken a hostile turn. She wanted me gone. I didn't blame her.

With reluctance, she said, "A boardinghouse on Blake Street's all Gert ever tol' me." She glanced up. "I swear."

"Everything you've said has been the truth, to the best of your memory. I know that."

The dining room door, through which Jules had exited, cracked open a few inches. "Best you bring them sandwiches, woman. The po-licemen is coming down from Miss Belinda's room."

I ripped a leaf from the notebook and wrote: *As advised, I've hied for home. JBS*

To Pansy, I said, "Do you remember the constable that arrived a moment before I did? A tall man in a black frock coat?"

"Yes'm."

"His name is Jack O'Shaughnessy. Will you please give him this message for me?"

Pansy slipped the ragged paper in her pocket, then

hefted the tray. Whether she heard my expression of thanks, I wasn't sure.

The mansion's service entrance had a brick walkway leading to a side drive partially overhung by a porte cochere. Beyond it was a sandstone block and clapboard stable. Lifting my skirts, I wandered across the lawn to the rear of the house.

Cows lowed in the pasture beyond, their night sounds less pronounced than the odor of fresh droppings. I jumped at voices raised in argument, then realized they were drifting from the front lawn, not closing in from behind me. From the overheard snatches, it seemed a constable was giving the reporter, Glover Rudd, a heave-ho out the front door. The French doors were closed, but the rope still hung from the balcony rail outside Belinda Abercrombie's bedchamber. To my dismay, crushed walnut hulls lined the flower beds adjacent to the exterior wall. In the darkness, it was impossible to tell whether the shrubbery had any broken branches. I dared not strike a match.

To my right, a shadow moved across a wan rectangle of light on the grass. I shrank back, peering up at the source. A silhouette loomed at the window in the room next to Mrs. Abercrombie's. By the height and shape, I surmised it to be Avilla. She couldn't see me, but it didn't keep my heart from pounding.

When I reached the buggy, Izzy was dozing, his head a-droop in the harness. An undertaker's wagon with black-draped isinglass side windows, a few saddled horses, and another buggy had joined the parked cavalcade.

Constable Hopkins stood guard at the entrance. The spectators had been shooed away or quit the scene of their own accord. I departed with more questions than answers.

As I'd expected and dreaded, Won Li was waiting up for me. Jack was the unknowing recipient of a series of Occidental insults for abandoning me to my own devices at such a late hour. Mentioning my obviously unscathed condition did naught to stem the tide. While I waited for Won Li to lose his voice, or a lung to collapse, I stoked the woodstove and put on the kettle. Rifling the pie safe devoted to his herbal pharmacy released fragrances both pleasing and noxious.

The long, complicated day had sapped my energy. Sleep was the sensible antidote, but there was research to be done, requiring a lively, agile brain. In addition, if Jack perchanced to retrieve his horse from our stable in the wee hours, slumbering through his visit would not achieve an informational exchange in regard to the Abercrombie case.

He'd proven himself egregiously tight-lipped about police matters. Coming at him from ambush and a subtle application of friendly enticement should alleviate that minor character flaw.

Won Li watched as I measured gotu kola, red clover, damiana, ginseng, kava kava, red raspberry, peppermint, and cloves in a teapot.

"Have you taken a chill?" he asked. "Or are you desirous of plowing a field by moonlight?"

I laughed. Changing out of my rumpled suit into my thinnest cotton gown before the elixir fired my blood was imperative. However, his remark confirmed I'd remembered the recipe correctly.

We took chairs at the kitchen's round, pine table, where I discoursed the rudiments of the LeBruton divorce and Abercrombie robbery/homicide. His interest was as plain as a spinster's shimmy, but he said, "Your father would not approve. *I* do not approve."

"Neither do I."

In my experience, no race of people on earth could scowl as menacingly as those of the Chinese persuasion.

"I do not approve of men who thrash women physically and emotionally," I said, "and I do not approve of a life being extinguished for a pillow slip full of jewelry.

"Furthermore, I don't give a fig whether what's happened to Penelope LeBruton and Belinda Abercrombie is my bailiwick, my duty, or my responsibility to resolve. They deserve a champion. I may not be equal to the task, but I can't turn my back and hope for the best."

Won Li folded his hands on the table. "That is not the type of disapproval to which I referred."

Steam flumed from the kettle's spout. "Oh, yes it is. Years ago, if I'd asked for approval before I jumped that yahoo and his friends who were beating you to a pulp, would I have gotten it?"

I took a pot holder from a wall peg, poured boiling water into the teapot, and shrouded it in a cozy. "I told you then, I can't hash bullies, cheaters, or drunks. All that's changed is adding killers and thieves to the list."

"Your motives are honorable, Joby. They have been for as long as I have known you. It is your methods that are too often impulsive and foolhardy."

I kissed the top of his shaven pate. "How many times have we had this argument?"

"If you will allow a rough estimate, I would say three thousand, four hundred and seventy-nine."

"Have you won one, yet?"

"The knowing enjoy water. The humane enjoy mountains."

I groaned. "Again, in English, please. I'm too tired to puzzle out Confucius's analects."

"Enjoy life. Take trouble as a challenge to overcome, but don't seek it."

"I do enjoy life and I've never sought trouble. It's just always had a way of finding me."

SIX

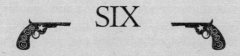

With my nose in a book was precisely how I wakened the next morning. I knew the instant my eyes opened that last night, while I'd been changing my clothes, Won Li had substituted a muscle-relaxing tea for the stimulant I'd brewed.

He'd also taken the precaution of not being in hollering range when I realized the treachery. Calling his name indoors and from the back porch was to no avail. I didn't comprehend the thoroughness of his disappearance until I finished my ablutions and ventured to the stable.

Izzy and the buggy were gone. In a second stall stood Loralei, Jack O'Shaughnessy's bay mare. He must have toiled deep into the morning hours, then collapsed on a cot at the station house.

Loralei had been unsaddled and curried to a glorious sheen. I fed her the cubed sugar intended for Izzy and wondered why my treasonous patron thought I'd stay to home, rather than take the liberty of borrowing Jack's trusty steed.

Since the age of four, I'd ridden bareback and saddle-mounted for the sheer joy of it, as well as transportation. One of Papa's few deviations from Victorian mores pertinent to feminine comportment was railing against the invention of the sidesaddle.

"It's a pretty seat, with a gal's skirts and petticoats all caped and aflutter in the breeze," he said, "but for practical purposes, it's as worthless as teats on a ladybug."

I tried it once, for the novelty and in keeping with my youthful theory that adult opinions were designed to wreck enjoyment of life to its fullest. Imagine my shock when Papa's judgment of female equestrianship proved accurate. A subsequent yarn about a secret garden where babies were plucked from under cabbage leaves restored my faithlessness in grown-ups.

Except now that I was past the age of majority, I cringed at thoughts of making a spectacle of myself—well, any oftener than necessity dictated. Unfortunately, a lady riding through town forking a saddle was liable to generate scorn from her own gender and impure thoughts from the opposite.

The only activity less comfortable and more awkward than riding sidesaddle on a sidesaddle was riding sidesaddle on tack designed for a man.

For one thing, a typical Western pommel is several inches shorter than its sidesaddle counterpart. Crooking my knee around the former provided as much bracing and balance as a fossilized mushroom and pinched the bejesus out of my calf, to boot. Add to that, the saddle's curvature created a sensation similar to my buttocks being wedged into a tinware dishpan that's bouncing down the world's longest set of stairs.

Aside from anatomical abuses inflicted in the name of convention, the brief ride into Denver City proper was uneventful—other than the heat wilting me like bacon fat drizzled over spinach leaves. A black cloche and jersey wool dress was mandatory attire for one of my appointed rounds, but criminitly, how I envied Asians their traditional white mourning garb.

As usual, my arrival at the agency wasn't met with clients queued up and clamoring to hire a professional investigator. I dialed the vault's combination and pushed down the brass handle. The door swung open on oiled hinges.

Papa's badge lay atop his holstered Colt revolver. There'd have been hell to pay if he'd been caught the night he'd reclaimed the tin-plated memento he'd slapped on Judge Story's desk that very afternoon.

As it happened, I was thrilled when Papa excused himself after supper to wet his whistle at his favorite Ft. Smith saloon. I gave him a ten-minute head start, then hopped bareback on the paint pony I owned at the time and lit out for the courthouse in Van Buren.

My father had bought and paid for that Deputy U.S. Marshal's badge with cash money, blood, sweat, and tears. Judge Story demanded it when Papa resigned, but I'd go to prison for life before I'd let that slimy carpetbagger keep it.

When I'd hoisted myself through the judge's office window, Papa had jumped higher than most would expect a six-foot-three-inch, two-hundred-pound lawdog was able. My heart had swelled bigger than the whole of me when I'd seen that tin star already clutched in his hand.

As far as I know, it was the only crime my father ever committed. Alas, the same couldn't be said of his daughter, even before the night of our accidental collusion.

I returned the pouch containing the agency's financial assets to the vault. Ten dollars and change remained. The balance tucked into my reticule would be spent. Whether for good or ill, I left to Providence.

Within the hour, Loralei conveyed me to the train depot's Western Union telegrapher. A host of like-worded telegrams from Joseph Beckworth Sawyer were dispatched to sheriffs and municipal police departments in California, Nevada, and Utah, all requesting an urgent reply.

I refused to believe Penelope was the first and only woman Rendal LeBruton had romanced for profit. Lotharios and bunco-steerers were made, not born. Criminals of all stripes were drawn to prosperous cities like lead to lodestone, and Abelia *had* said Rendal met Penelope in San Francisco.

If my hunch was correct, grounds for a speedy, uncontestable dissolution were virtually guaranteed.

Blake Street was next on my itinerary. There were some blocks where one's virtue, wallet, or life were endangered even in daylight. However, a gardener with a penchant for gambling probably did not frequent the avenue's tonier reaches.

The initials D.P.D. were etched and whitened on both aspects of Loralei's saddle skirt. Only a certified lunatic would unhitch and abscond with a horse belonging to a city constable. Naturally, I excluded myself from that group.

Sam Merck, groundskeeper and suspect in the Abercrombie homicide, was no stranger to mixologists at the Green Flag, Strange & Knaught, May Flower, and Green

Bement's saloons. William Marchant's Billiard Hall, the Atlantic Garden, and Planter's House were also waystops along Merck's road to perdition. It was disappointing, but not unexpected, that none I spoke with at those establishments would confide Merck's address to his recently widowed sister.

I couldn't feature a boardinghouse more filthy than the second I braved until I smelled its downstreet competitor. The structure's whomperjawed front door was screened, but flies buzzed in and out of the building's unchinked log walls.

A toothless, fat man rocking on the stoop had no use for soap or the spittoon beside him. He smiled at me. The cold biscuit I'd gobbled for breakfast did a do-si-do in my stomach. I kept my distance, but any locale west of the Mississippi River was too near.

I bid him a good morning and inquired after Sam Merck.

"Who wants to know?"

"I'm his sister. My husband just passed away—"

"What you want Sam for?"

"Then he *does* board here?"

"Nope." A stream of tobacco joined its predecessors swamping the base of the spittoon. "Not no more, he don't. The sumbitch done packed up his plunder in the dead of night."

"Last night?"

"Yep. Owes me two weeks for the room, too." He scratched what itched. "Promised he'd pay up this morning. Comin' into money, he told me. He ain't never got that far in arrears afore, so I took him at his word."

One eye squinted shut. "I don't reckon you're good for it, are ya?"

"No."

"Hmmph. I figgered as much."

"How long did Sam live here?"

"You sure ask a lot of questions. Even for a widder-lady."

I chuckled in spite of myself. The landlord was as repulsive as a bloated toad, but he had a certain charm.

"Oh, I 'spect Sam bunked here three, mebbe four months. Didn't leave so much as a watch fob to pawn for what's due me."

His eyes rambled my length, the orbs acting independently of each other. It was mesmerizing for its ocular impossibility. "Merck ain't dead, is he?"

"I can't say with certainty, but I doubt it." I thanked him for his time and started away. He called after me, "If you see him, or that Gertie he runs with, tell 'em I wants my money, cash on the barrelhead."

I turned. "Would that be Gertrude Hiss?"

"Never heared her Christian name. Not that I'd peg 'er for no Sunday school teacher." His belly jiggled when he laughed. "Them two romped hosannas out'n the bedsprings, though. From what Gertie hollered, 'twas always a helluva prayer meetin' goin' on in there."

A blush blossomed at my stockinged toes and raced to my crown. It hadn't abated when I entered the bakery between E and F streets. I took some solace in the ruddiness of owner Adolph Schinner's jowled countenance, though its color was an occupational hazard.

Come to think of it, so was mine.

I cursed Won Li with blistering fervor as I remounted Loralei sideward, balancing a string-tied, pasteboard box on my winged knee. The bay craned her neck and neighed at my sudden fidgeting for purchase.

"Go easy, girl. Heaven forbid, the Abercrombies be scandalized by me riding like a human to bear them a condolence cake."

A Mexican boy of about twelve was repairing the damage done to the flower beds by last night's Looby Lu's. In heavily accented English, he told me his name was Ferdi and that Sam Merck hadn't reported for work that morning. Avilla had waited a full hour before hiring Ferdi and his brother, Santo, to replace the groundskeeper.

I was midway to the door when I stopped short and whirled around. Pansy's description of Sam Merck and Gertrude Hiss chimed in my mind. *That's* where I'd seen them. A stocky redhead with a mannish hairstyle and her disreputable companion had been among the rubberneckers on the lawn last night. They'd rated notice for standing on the fountain's far side, separate from the others.

Why had they stayed outside, rather than go into the house? Now Sam Merck was absent from his job. Six bits said Gert wasn't ricing potatoes for pancakes in the kitchen, either.

A mourning wreath hung from each door, and the windows were draped in black bunting. Even without them, an aura of tragedy was almost palpable.

Jules, dressed in a butler's livery, answered the bell. His eyes were swollen to slits and his shoulders looked as though anvils weighted them. He accepted the boxed raisin cake and said, "Mister Abercrombie isn't receivin' till after the service for Miss Belinda."

"Might Avilla Abercrombie be receiving?"

"Miss Avilla, she isn't here. Had things needing took care of before the funeral. The master's too sick at heart to do them hisself."

His monotone took me aback. If his lips hadn't moved,

I'd wonder if a ventriloquist was hiding behind the door. "Are you all right, Jules?"

He hesitated, then set the box aside and stepped out, pulling the door after him. "No, ma'am. I never been so scared in all my born days. Pansy, too."

"Scared? Why?"

"Those po-licemens was here till past daybreak. Looked high, low and in-betwixt for Miss Belinda's jewelry. After they tore through the house, they tramped the yard with lanterns. One even fished a stick around in the outhouse."

He wiped his face with a handkerchief from his trousers' pocket. "They think we's the burglars. Think we stole from them other folks, too."

I squeezed his forearm. It was as pliant as an iron pipe. "They're just being thorough, Jules."

"If that was all of it, I might ought to agree with you. Pansy, she heard two of 'em talkin' whilst they ransacked our room. One of 'em said I must have given the loot to a . . . a 'complice—yeah, that's it. Said 'twas the people in the buggy I sent after the police."

The thought hadn't crossed my mind, but it was a logical suspicion. Actually, it would be a brilliant ruse to divert suspicion. "Didn't Mister Abercrombie tell the constables he sent you to get help?"

Jules shook his head. "The master don't remember keen enough to swear to it. Miss Avilla don't, either. They're sure they must have, seein' as how somebody *did* tell the police, 'cept whoever it was, run into the station house and out again and didn't give a name."

"You didn't recognize the people in the buggy?"

"No, ma'am. There was two of 'em and they was white. That's the onliest thing I recollect."

Miss Cornucopia Brown, a teacher imported from West Virginia to Ft. Smith for one school term, had been wild for an exercise she'd called a lightning quiz. She'd belt out spelling words, history questions, sums and the like for us to answer with whatever first popped into our heads.

I won enough horehound candy to turn my stomach, but hearing Bubba John Vickery blurting state capitals and the names of Columbus's ships was a pure-de-miracle. Miss Brown said the brain is like a frog in a pan of water on the stove. Ponder too long, and it won't matter if *jump* is the correct answer.

"You said there were two people in the buggy."

Jules nodded.

"Two men?"

"Huh-uh. A man and a woman."

"Old? Young?"

"The man was older'n her. Coulda been her daddy."

"Was she blonde?"

"No, her hair was brown as molasses." He hesitated a beat. "And the gent had one of them billy goat beards."

"A Vandyke?"

He shrugged. "Could be the fancy name for it. I don't rightly know."

"What color was the horse?"

" 'Twas—" Jules reared back his head. "How is it I'm rememberin' things I don't recollect payin' any mind to?"

"The horse. What color was it?"

"They's palominos. A pair of 'em. One too many, for a gaddin' about town, if'n you ask me."

I agreed. "You didn't tell the police any of those details?"

"No, ma'am. All I recalled was two people in a buggy, till you pecked them other things out of me."

Miss Cornucopia Brown would delight in his choice of words. I said, "It might be wise to tell the police what you've remembered. If that couple can be found—"

"Aw, it won't do no good now, Miz Sawyer. If they didn't believe me last night, they'll just say I made it up to look more like the master *did* tell me to get help."

I had no argument. It was a shame that whoever interrogated him last night hadn't attended school in Ft. Smith. "And Pansy's corroboration doesn't count, because she's your wife."

"Nope . . . if you mean her swearin' the master sent me don't make for a hill o' beans." He snorted. "Miss Avilla give the constables the sharp side of her tongue for actin' like there's blood on our hands, but they didn't heed her, neither."

My own objectivity was faulty and I knew it. I should have, but didn't, view Pansy or Jules as possible suspects, before or after our postmortem interview in the kitchen.

The police obviously did. In their parlance, the crime might be a put-up, meaning the perpetrator ingratiated himself with a servant, or enticed assistance for a share of the loot.

Jules's lengthy attachment to Hubert Abercrombie could mean his loyalty was unimpeachable or that resentments had festered over the years, kindling a hunger for revenge.

His current anxiety seemed genuine, but was it rooted in fear of an unjust arrest and conviction, or fear that the truth will out?

Had the now three-time, professional burglar resorted to murder when Belinda Abercrombie caught him in the act? Or was the constabulary right about a put-up job, but mistaken about Jules and/or Pansy's involvement?

"Did Gertrude Hiss come home last night?"

Jules's brow knitted, as though trying to place the name. He then declared, "Ain't seen hide nor hair of her, since supper, last. Now Pansy's got to cook *and* do the maidin' chores." He jerked a thumb toward Ferdi. "I'd guess you already know Sam Merck is gone, too."

"Gone?" I repeated. "What makes you say that?"

"Well, he ain't here, is he?"

"Yes, but the gambling halls Merck patronized were far from genteel. An accident could have befallen him and Gertrude Hiss. Why, for all anyone knows, they could have eloped—"

"Today of all days?" Rue inflected Jules's chuckle. "The po-lice sacked Gert's room, same as ours, but I don't see 'em layin' blame at her feet, nor Sam's."

No, I thought, but you certainly are.

He pushed the door open a crack, listened, then pulled it almost closed again. "I can't tarry much longer. What I come out to ask was about that big Irish cop what was here last night. Pansy 'tol me you and him are friends."

I nodded.

"Them other two didn't believe nothin' me and her said. Your friend, though, he listened respectful-like, the same as you did."

Little did Jules know, Jack O'Shaughnessy had also noted every twitch, aversion of the eyes, and inconsistency during questioning.

"He didn't ask," Jules went on, "and with all the hulla-baloo, we forgot to say, but Miss Belinda was fit as a fiddle yesterday till a spell past dinnertime."

His insinuation was clear, but I plastered on a befud-dled expression.

"Don't you think that Irishman ought to know that we

all ate the same food, but nobody else took sick on Gert's cookin'. The only one that did, we're layin' to rest this afternoon."

I checked the impulse to argue that Belinda Abercrombie had been strangled, not poisoned. If Gertrude Hiss was the inside informant, why would she kibosh the Abercrombies' engagement with the Estabrooks?

Ye gods and little fishes. That applied as equally to Gert and Sam Merck as conspirators, as it did to Pansy and Jules. And neither ruled out the mysterious Good Samaritans as accomplices. But then which or whom had robbed the McCoynes and Whitelaws?

After again contorting into a makeshift sidesaddle position, I surveyed the sky, feeling very small and wishing for a vision of Papa's face in the rack of broken clouds. A wink would sustain me. A thunderhead would take the slump from my spine. In my muddled mind, I heard him laugh and say, "There's more to being an Indian princess than poking eagle feathers in a headband and whooping to beat hell."

I'll swan, Papa's health may have suffered since his demise, but somehow, he was getting smarter with each passing day.

I spurred Loralei with my one available heel. There was more to being a private investigator than gilt letters arced on a storefront window, too. Princess or detective, maybe playacting was all I was cut out to do.

Self-doubt colored my demeanor a proper shade of aggrieved when I called at the Estabrook estate. A titian-haired countrywoman of Jack O'Shaughnessy's showed me to a morning room off the grand hall.

I seated myself in a velvet-upholstered chair by the fireplace, for fear a misdrawn breath would precipitate an avalanche. An invading militia could lurk behind the room's forest of potted banana palms, hibiscus, and ferns. Gimcracks by the score cramped every horizontal surface, including the hearth. Posed on layered Turkish and Armenian rugs, a litter of ceramic pug dogs ogled me as though lunch were overdue and they might be compelled to fend for themselves.

Ornate clutter was all the rage, but the room's superabundance of clocks had me praying Jesus I'd vacate the premises before they tolled the hour.

Elise Estabrook was a handsome woman whose regal carriage belied her advanced years. Hands clasped in front of her, she scrutinized me through a pair of half-spectacles. "My maid tells me you're investigating Belinda Abercrombie's death."

Before I could respond, she went on, "On whose behalf, Miss Sawyer?"

"I keep my clients' names in strictest confidence."

Especially, I thought, when I don't have one. As I'd told Won Li, Belinda Abercrombie deserved justice. Somewhere between her home and the Estabrooks' parlor, I'd realized how desperately I needed to prove to myself and everyone else that I was capable of delivering it.

"Well," Elise said, "I suppose there's no harm in telling you what I told the police . . ."

I pulled back my shoulders. "My confidentiality also extends to those involved in a case under investigation, Mrs. Estabrook."

A slender eyebrow rose in amusement. "You do have the jargon down pat, don't you?" She removed her eyeglasses and tapped them on her chin. "Hubert Abercrombie and my husband are friends and business associates—precious ore, real estate investments and the like.

"Belinda Abercrombie and I detest each other. She has—*had*—the social graces and intellect of a chimpanzee. Hubert, of course, was besotted with her beauty and, shall we say, willingness to please."

"Did she love him?"

"Hmmm. What an odd question." Elise traced a statue of a moon goddess, then examined her fingertip for dust. "Yes, I think she did, in her own way."

"And Avilla?"

"Poor child. She was only six when she lost her real mother during a cholera outbreak. Barely thirteen when Hubert introduced Belinda as his new wife—a fait accompli, as it were.

"To be fair, Belinda was very sweet to Avilla. I can't say she was necessarily a *mother* to her, but perhaps that was for the best. There wasn't much age difference between them, you know."

It was obvious my hostess was a thespian at heart. She relished being center stage, even in her own hideously overdecorated parlor. When I asked about the cancelled dinner party, Elise said, "It was typical of Belinda to wait until the last minute to send regrets." She flinched. "You must think I'm a terrible shrew, but I was relieved when her note arrived. Witty repartee is not only wasted on a dolt, it's perfectly exhausting. How was *I* to know the evening was to be her last on earth?"

I stifled a grin. The woman's lack of reserve was refreshing. "I appreciate your candor, Mrs. Estabrook."

She tossed her head. "I'm somewhat notorious for it, I'm afraid."

"Were other guests in attendance?"

"No. The men had business to discuss after dinner and I planned to develop an excruciating headache if they closeted themselves in the library too long."

She raised a hand, palm out. "To answer your next question, Durwin, my husband, and Hubert are concerned that the government may follow Europe's adoption of an exclusive gold standard and suspend the coinage of silver. It's politics as usual and as boring as bird-watching, but men must have some excuse to puff on cigars and puff out their chests."

"Mrs. Estabrook?"

Elise looked up at the maid standing in the doorway. "Thank you, Neva. I'll be along after I show Miss Sawyer out." Turning to me, she added graciously, "Unless you have more questions?"

I shook my head. "You've been most generous with your time, Mrs. Estabrook."

"I wish I had more of it. Fresh ears for stale blather are always welcome." She rested a hand on the doorknob. "Are you attending the funeral this afternoon?"

I'd chosen a black ensemble for my condolence call on Avilla and Hubert Abercrombie, unaware the rites for the recently departed Belinda would be held so soon. Jules mentioned the funeral, but I'd assumed Avilla was out making arrangements for tomorrow, not today.

"I will, if my afternoon appointment doesn't interfere."

Elise said, "This rush to burial is positively scandalous, but I'm sure this ghastly heat is responsible. In any event, I think the ritual of sitting a vigil with the dead is beyond macabre. I've already told Durwin to plant me before I'm cold. If he displays my corpse in the front room, I'll haunt him till the end of his days."

SEVEN

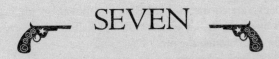

Izzy and the again driverless buggy were parked outside the agency. Jack O'Shaughnessy sat in the narrow awning of shade the building afforded. A basket lay at his feet. He was gnawing on a piece of fried chicken.

"You're eating my lunch."

"You stole my horse."

"One has nothing to do with the other."

"Does, too." Jack's mouth curved up in a greasy grin. "Spending half the livelong day walking from pillar to post makes a man plumb famished."

I waved at the buggy. "Izzy walked. You rode."

"No, ma'am. The buggy was here before I was."

Won Li must have left it and my lunch and hotfooted it home. The coward.

I pried my leg from the pommel and slid off the saddle without assistance. A bummer strolling the opposite side of Champa saluted my alacrity. At least, I preferred to think that was the cause and not the indecent length of stockinged limbs I'd exposed.

Reticule extracted from the saddlebag, I picked my way round the fly-blown souvenirs of continuous oxen, horse, and mule traffic. Soot and fine ash belched from factories skimmed the roofs of tall buildings. Denver City was a beautiful metropolis as long as pedestrians didn't look up, down, or inhale.

Jack carried the basket inside and put it on my desk. "I'll have you know, I didn't eat but half what's in there, and I didn't touch the pie."

Without bothering to smooth my skirts under me, I collapsed in the chair. "Your restraint is admirable. Won Li makes the best fried chicken in the Territory."

Jack rested a hip on the corner of the desk. He looked haggard and tetchy around the edges. "Holding my appetite in check pales in comparison to the restraint I showed at the Abercrombies last night."

I made a face. "Did I interfere? Did I leave the house in a timely, discreet fashion?"

"Yes. And no. I'll give you discreet, but timely would have been when I told you to vamoose. As for interfering, you did that first step you took into the house."

I threw up my arms in exasperation. "You're just being difficult."

"I'm trying to keep you from getting hurt. Or worse." He chafed his hands. "A second-story man is one thing, darlin'. The line between stealing and murder is one most burglars will go to jail for before they'll cross it."

"I know. That's what bothers me about this whole case."

"Well, it isn't bothering you enough. Killer-thieves are first cousins to bank robbers. They go in with their minds already made up to take lives to spare their own. That's why they're about the most dangerous hombres a lawman'll ever come up against."

Jack translated my gesture correctly. From the basket, he removed a jar half-full of apple cider and twisted off the lid. The juice had lost its chill but quenched my thirst.

I set the jar on the blotter. "Why Belinda Abercrombie? Why did the thief unleash his wrath on her? No one was harmed in the earlier robberies."

"The other folks weren't at home at the time. If they had been, or walked in on it . . ."

I shuddered at the implication. "Are you saying all three robberies were the same, other than the murder at the Abercrombie home?"

Jack nodded. "Using a string of fake pearls for a garrote makes an ugly sort of sense. The killer grabbed what was close at hand."

"The pearls were imitation?"

"Yeah, but expensive imitations."

"Did Belinda own any strands of real pearls?"

Jack took a sheet of paper from his coat pocket. "Two, according to the list of missing jewelry Avilla wrote out for us."

"How many fake strings?"

His eyes traveled the length of the paper and up again. "Just the one, I guess. There's costume pieces on here, too, but no mention of another imitation necklace."

A sour taste coated my mouth. It wasn't the residue of pressed apples. "Jules thinks you suspect him and Pansy."

"The butler did it?" Jack laughed. "Constable Hopkins was fawnching for an inside job, too. It'd wrap things up with a tidy bow, except he can't explain how Jules and Pansy pulled off the earlier robberies."

"Accomplices?"

In a tone suggesting the sun had scalded my brain, he replied, "Oh, so they hired outside help at the McCoynes and the Whitelaws, then messed in their own backyard at the Abercrombies? While the family was *home?*"

I hadn't been fond of the premise, but it was deserving of consideration. "I'm guessing you've overruled the possibility of them hiding in plain sight."

"Nothing's been ruled out, darlin'." Jack rolled a shoulder and groaned. Sleeping facedown on a law book was better than no sleep at all. "Nothing will be, till an arrest is made."

"Yes, but does the 'messing in their own backyard' argument include Gertrude Hiss and Sam Merck? I happen to have my own theory about them. If you're interested."

"Talk fast. The chief, the mayor, the newspapers, and every nabob in town is screaming for swift justice. Until we've got a suspect in the hoosegow, nobody on the force gets as much as an hour's leave."

I'd scanned the *Rocky Mountain News* banner headline when I replaced the edition on Papa's desk that morning. DEATH STALKS DENVER CITY. SOCIALITE ROBBED AND MURDERED IN HER OWN HOME. The substance of the articles, I left to imagination. Doubtless the reporters applied liberal doses of theirs when composing them.

"What if Gertrude and Sam planned to rob the Abercrombies while they were dining with the Estabrooks? When Belinda fell ill, they were so cocky about getting away with the earlier crimes they decided against a delay."

"Mighty risky," Jack said.

"Any riskier than Sam dodging all the people he owed money to? Saloon owners. Gamblers. His landlord?" I snapped my fingers. "Who, by the by, told me that Sam said he was coming into some money and would pay his back rent today."

Jack's jaw fell, then snapped shut. "God smite me for a fool. I should have known it was you sashaying up and down Blake Street telling everyone you were Merck's widowed sister."

Mustering poise wasn't effortless, particularly in light of the spasm suddenly afflicting Jack's temple and the corner of his left eye. How peculiar. From time to time, my father had been plagued by a similar tic.

"I'm sure you'll agree, I couldn't introduce myself as a detective. Not a soul would have talked to me if I had."

Jack pushed off the desk. Sputtering gave way to arm motions common to a circus fire walker. "Mary, Mother of us all. How's this for a what-if? What if Merck is our man? Or he's in league with the killer? How long do you think it'll take for him to divine who you are and shut you up permanently?"

"Pshaw. For what earthly reason would anyone want to kill me?"

"Present company excluded?" Jack cleared his throat. "One, you're too danged nosy for your own good. Two, we have no idea who the killer is and he has no idea whether you're a threat or not. It's smarter to get rid of you than take the chance. Three, if a couple of those hard cases you pestered believe you're Merck's sister and know he has a king's ransom in jewelry stashed somewhere, they might use you to get to him. When they find you aren't, what do you reckon they'll do? Apologize for the inconvenience and take you home?"

"Oh." I squirmed and looked away.

Mentioning the greater likelihood of being keelhauled

by a freight-wagon than kidnapped by brigands presented a sore lack of diplomacy. So did insisting I'd taken care of myself quite handily with fists and firearms since I was knee-high to a short stump.

Jack gripped the chair's arms and loomed over me, his face was at once solemn and tender and very near mine. "You're one of a kind, Miz Joby Sawyer. I've never known another woman quite like you."

"Are you complimenting me or praying for salvation?"

"A little of each, I'd reckon."

Kiss me, I thought. I double-dog dare you. Not one of those granny pecks on the cheek you're so inclined toward, either. A true, full on the lips, sockdolager of a first kiss to prove that mouth of yours is good for something besides nattering at me.

"I know firsthand the evil some men are capable of, with no more thought than they'd give to slapping a mosquito," he said.

"So do I." My gaze averted to his neck, which I could easily curl my arm around, pull him close and kiss *him* till his toes bunched so tight in his boots that he'd be hobbled for a minute or ten.

Who wrote the rules saying men had all the liberties at their disposal and women were obliged to dither and stew, waiting for them to take one, if and when the damn fools ever shut up long enough to get crackin'.

"I'm asking you," he said, "plain as I know how, if you have an ounce of caring for me, don't go chasing after the devil's own."

He wanted to kiss me as much as I wanted him to. His eyes were heavy lidded and the irises as deep blue as sapphires. But I wouldn't make a promise I was sure to break, just for the glory of feeling Jack's lips on mine.

I could have said if he cared for *me*, he wouldn't issue ultimatums. Won Li worried incessantly about my safety and, in all honesty, for good and sufficient reason, but never once had he demanded an emotional kind of ransom from me.

Putting voice to those sentiments was as futile as herding ducks to a desert. To reverse Jack's ultimatum by saying if he loved me he'd accept me for who I am was fighting hypocrisy with hypocrisy.

Jack straightened and strode out the door. Through the window, I watched him unwrap Loralei's reins from the rail. When he rode away, his profile was as abstracted as a cut-paper silhouette.

It was half past two when Garret McCoyne and Avery Whitelaw arrived. I was preparing to finish my law book research in the comfort of home when the tall and short of them darkened my door.

McCoyne glared at the opposite half of my desk. "Mr. Sawyer isn't here."

"No. He isn't."

"We had an appointment."

I stacked the books that had only served as ballast since I departed the house that morning. McCoyne's apparent opinion that he left outhouses smelling like rose gardens inspired an adroit comeback. "Had my father made an appointment with you, would you have dallied half an hour for *him* to make an appearance?"

The banker consulted his pocketwatch. The mine owner shifted uncomfortably. "You're Mr. Sawyer's daughter?"

I nodded. Avery Whitelaw seemed a decent sort. Not as cockapert by far as McCoyne.

"Did Sawyer send you in his stead to the Abercrombies

with the police?" McCoyne inquired. "Daughter or not, we thought you were just a clerk."

My smile would have caused a rattler to seek the nearest hole in the ground. "Then you thought wrong, didn't you?"

"No insult meant," Whitelaw said. "It's the first I've ever heard of a woman investigator."

"Well, that truly is a surprise. Kate Warne was a Pinkerton operative from 1856 until her death two years ago. She was credited with saving President-elect Lincoln from an assassination plot during the inauguration."

"You don't say." Whitelaw's chin rumpled. "It's said that Allan Pinkerton stops at nothing to get his man. A real bulldog of a detective."

Who rather resembled one as well, I thought. The Scotsman was a cooper by trade until he rafted to a tiny island for lumber and happened upon a nest of counterfeiters. After a short stint as the lone detective on the Chicago police force, then a Special United States Mail Agent, Pinkerton founded his own agency and its slogan, "We Never Sleep."

I gathered up my bag, books, and two days' luncheon baskets. "If you'll excuse me, gentlemen, I have an appointment of my own to keep."

They stood gaping at me, as though gut-shot but disinclined to fall down. Garret McCoyne removed an envelope from an inner jacket pocket. "If you'll spare us a moment of your time, I believe it'll be worth your while."

As present company's sole representative of a well-mannered upbringing, I resettled my cargo on the desk.

McCoyne passed the envelope to Avery Whitelaw, who pushed it beside my reticule. "There's a bank draft inside, payable in the amount of one hundred dollars to Sawyer Investigations."

"A retainer," McCoyne said, "for services, plus expenses."

Composure is exceedingly difficult to maintain when one's feet are tapping to dance a merry jig. A hundred dollars was a blooming fortune, in my estimation. The agency's till had winnowed to a week's remove from insolvency and my alternative employment as a shopgirl.

I clasped my hands together, lest one or the other take a notion to snatch up the envelope and deposit it beyond the reach of a gentleman's grasp. "What service are you so eager for Sawyer Investigations to provide?"

"Doubtless, you're aware that our respective homes were burgled," McCoyne said, "and the thief absconded with thousands of dollars in jewelry."

"All I know of the crimes is what I've read in the newspapers."

Whitelaw said, "Several of the pieces are irreplaceable because of the sentimental value attached. A brooch handed down from my wife's grandmother, for example. It was to be presented to our eldest daughter on her wedding day, as it has been for three generations."

"My wife is virtually inconsolable," McCoyne said. "She's been under a doctor's care since the robbery. I have the resources to buy the woman her own blasted jewelry store, but oh, no. Nothing will do but recovering what was lost."

What a coldhearted twit. Had it never occurred to him that at least *his* wife was still drawing breath? Whitelaw's plea had evoked a modicum of sympathy. McCoyne's spawned contempt.

To him, I inquired, "If your wife's trove was so valuable, why wasn't it locked in a safe?"

"It should have been." He looked at Whitelaw. "We

each have them, but our wives developed inexcusable habits of removing pieces to wear, then 'forgetting' to return them afterward."

Whitelaw stammered, "Margaret and I never dreamed a thief would climb in a second-floor window. Not with four children and a houseful of servants!"

McCoyne's question usurped my own. "Then why go to the expense of installing a vault?" He waved a dismissal. "Such is the constables' favorite riddle. My wife has yet to manufacture a rational answer."

My gaze fell to the envelope. U.S. Deputy Marshals for the Western District of Arkansas patrolled a seventy-four-thousand-square-mile area to earn a two-dollar fee, plus mileage, for each outlaw arrested. Papa would have had to fill a jail cheek-to-jowl for that kind of money.

"So, you want to hire the agency to catch the burglar and return your property."

"Well, I won't speak for Avery, but whether or not the thief is apprehended makes scant difference to me." McCoyne harrumphed. "Not that I wouldn't like to see him in leg-irons. If I had to choose, however, restoring my wife's jewelry collection takes precedence over identifying and punishing the guilty party."

"Really." Intuition's internal hum grew louder. I looked him straight in the eye. "I find your attitude a mite peculiar. Most robbery victims would choose the opposite."

The banker reddened. "The police are paid to arrest criminals. They spend little, if any, time searching for stolen goods, be it livestock or precious gems."

"Will you help us, Miss Sawyer?" Avery said. "Along with the bank draft is a list and description of the missing jewelry to aid your search. If your father requires a larger retainer, we'll pay whatever he asks."

Though I had no idea where to begin, or how to go about it, tracking down two pillow slips full of baubles wasn't the same as trifling with thieves, much less killers. On that point, Jack O'Shaughnessy, my bullheaded Irish white knight, would have to agree.

He wouldn't. He'd argue against the compromise in a most strenuous manner. Assuming I ever saw him again.

I picked up the envelope. The wax seal was etched with Garret McCoyne's copperplate initials. A hundred dollars. Lord only knew when, or if, my fingers would close around that amount of money again.

Whitelaw would be grateful for my efforts, whether the brooch and other geegaws were returned in whole, or part. McCoyne would be a tyrant to work for. He wouldn't be satisfied with anything less than complete success. If that.

If you have an ounce of caring for me, don't go out looking for the devil's own.

I won't, I promised Jack silently. I'll settle for having one as a client.

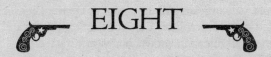

EIGHT

The funeral for Belinda Abercrombie consisted of a parlor service, followed by the Episcopalian custom of a second requiem at the graveside.

I chose to attend only the latter. It struck me as disrespectful to pay homage to the deceased, her husband, and stepdaughter and simultaneously scrutinize the mourners by invading the privacy of the Abercrombie home.

It was true as well that others even more desirous of relative invisibility than I also had a lesser chance of rating notice at the cemetery.

I joined the tag end of the processional, then hastened from the buggy to meld with the stream of people walking slowly toward the open grave. Beside it was a skirted platform where the casket would rest during the service.

As funerals are the apogee of chivalrous behavior, fading into the background wasn't a matter of discreet sidles and reverse trajectories. A bird's-eye view of my circumambulations must have resembled the L-shaped movements of a chessboard's knight. At long last, I stationed myself on the fringes beside a dwarf spice bush. Blotting perspiration from my face and neck with a hankie was not only compulsory but it also disguised my roving eyes.

By my estimate, the attendance was close to a hundred people. City officials and the cream of Denver City society milled with Abercrombie Department Store clerks and the requisite ghouls a violent death always attracted.

Being a member of none of those groups, I couldn't identify many attendants by name. Their height and lack thereof, haberdashery, and parasols deployed for shade didn't aid the process one iota. Clothing and demeanor were relied on to segregate the acquaintances from employees and the morbidly curious.

And the authorities. Or authority, as it were. I'd expected to see Jack or Hopkins or both, but it was the third, unmet constable from the murder scene who'd materialized on the other side of the shrub.

He was younger than I remembered. Sandy-haired, barrel-chested and dressed in street clothes. I smiled. He didn't return it.

Jules brought Hubert Abercrombie to the grave site in a wheeled chair. The widower acknowledged no one, staring ahead as though in a trance. Avilla walked alongside, holding her father's hand. A heavy veil obscured her face, but her posture was slumped and her step as leaden as a woman thrice her age.

Pallbearers wearing black sashes carried the rosewood casket to the platform. Garret McCoyne was the only one I recognized through a sudden blur of tears.

The most detestable kind of resentment roiled up inside me and fouled my mouth. I was blind to the mourners and deaf to the minister's Scripture reading.

What manner of fairness was there in the likes of Belinda Abercrombie being laid to rest in a gleaming coffin with fancy brass handles and corner braces? At his own peril, Joseph Beckworth Sawyer had rid The Nations of blackguards, killers, and all manner of human predators, while raising a child from infancy to adulthood, only to go to the ground swaddled in a dusty, moth-riddled blanket.

No preacher had read Psalm 121 over Papa. No army of mourners gathered round clutching roses to place on his grave. There was no one to weep and pray for a fine, brave, loving man's immortal soul, save his heartbroken daughter and the middle-aged Chinaman who loved Joe B. Sawyer like a brother.

Waves of grief swelled and washed over me. The harder I tried not to cry, the thicker and faster the tears coursed down my cheeks. I squinted up at the sky, telling myself that Papa was in a better place, but damn me for selfish, I wanted him back in the here and now.

Control was slow to come and slippery to hold on to, but I listened to the minister's final prayer asking the Lord for the strength and the wisdom to celebrate a life well lived, rather than dwell on Belinda's passage from it.

Jules pushed Hubert nearer the casket. The widower rose from his seat and murmured softly over it, his hand caressing the polished wood. A bouquet of white lilies and peach roses was laid upon it, then he bent and kissed the lid.

I looked away before I dissolved into tears again. The male onlookers stood as rigid as the granite monuments

surrounding us. If women were blessed with one free-
dom, it was to let their sorrow show on the outside, instead of bottling it up like carbonated soda in a lidded
shaker.

A glimpse of shorn, carrot-orange hair had me blink-
ing to clear my vision. Its owner's coal scuttle bonnet was
flapping in the breeze, granting peeks at the fiery strands
at her brow. I couldn't see the man beside her for a taller,
portly gent standing slightly behind him.

Pushing up on the balls of my feet and craning my
neck brought a new impediment into view—namely, the
statuesque figure of Elise Estabrook. I backpedaled a step
before she saw me. The tactic completely obliterated the
woman I believed to be Gertrude Hiss, but as the mourners moved to file past the bier, an opening revealed a
jump-seat wagonette drawn by matched palominos.

Great Caesar's ghost. Why couldn't I have been born a
twin, as the granny-woman predicted? Like most only
children, I'd wished for a playmate almost as often as for a
blameable surrogate when schemes went awry. Had
Mama begat me in duplicate, the need to be two places at
once wouldn't have posed a dilemma.

The wagonette's driver was a grizzled codger whose
dark sack coat added a touch of formality to his dunga-
rees and checkered shirt. To my left, the bonneted woman
was easing from the queue, preparing to insinuate herself
with a group about to cattycorner across the lawn in the
opposite direction.

The constable was surveying the assemblage in a general manner. I presumed he'd been assigned to detect a
burglar in its midst, as though the thief would attend
dressed in the black cowled cape and trousers portrayed
in the morning newspaper's illustration.

There wasn't time to explain the significance of the gold-colored team, which I was certain the constable had no knowledge of. With a final glance at the departing bonnet, I tugged on the cop's sleeve.

"I know Gertrude Hiss is wanted for questioning in the Abercrombie case," I said.

He nodded.

"See the people over there leaving the service? I think the woman in the gray bonnet is her. There's every chance Sam Merck is with her."

"You *think* so, eh?" He grinned. "Lieutenant O'Shaughnessy warned me about you, Miss Sawyer. Said you were as clever as they come."

I twisted the fabric of his coat sleeve, rather than the enticingly plump lobe of his jug-ear. "This is not a trick. I am a private detective. I have no authority to detain anyone for any reason. If you allow the Abercrombies' cook and, possibly, the gardener to sashay off to the train depot, the next thing Lieutenant O'Shaughnessy will hear is my screaming, vitriolic report of your complete and total incompetence."

The constable blanched so pale his freckles evaporated. "Yes, ma'am. Sorry, ma'am." He wrenched his sleeve from my grip. "If that's who they are, I'll nab 'em, right quick."

While he rushed off in one direction, I hastened in the other. Some people had paused for chitchat en route to their buggies. The majority was scattering like shotgun pellets.

The wagonette driver was poised to giddap the team as soon as a male passenger climbed into the rig's boxy cab and took his seat. I couldn't run. To do so would be an unforgivable insult. Limbs churning like pistons, I waved at the driver, as if hailing a hack for a ride.

He looked over his shoulder and spoke to his passenger. Keep talking, I pleaded. Do palaver at length on the rudeness of leaving an unescorted woman to fend for herself at the cemetery after a funeral service.

A few yards separated us when the driver faced around. His expression was sheepish as he apologized, then said, "I'm already hired, ma'am. If'n you'd care to wait, I can come back for you, soon as I'm able."

"That's very kind of you, but it's your horses that captured my eye. I simply had to hurry over for a closer look at such magnificent animals."

"They're pretty things, all right. I've tried to buy 'em a dozen times, but the owner won't sell." He turned. "Will ya, Mr. LeBruton?"

My heart stopped, then careered to my boots. The man in back leaned forward, a smile gleaming white in contrast to his Vandyke beard. "I should, in light of the exorbitant sum Mr. Orman charges to board them."

His smile widened. "But as you can see, miss, the team matches my wife's beautiful spun-gold hair."

Huddled in the corner of the rig, Penelope LeBruton stared at me through a flocked veil with such an expression of terror that I felt as though a pillow had been clamped over my face. Wrenching my eyes from her, I stammered, "Yes, yes, they do. Perfectly."

LeBruton's gaze meandered the length of me, tarrying at my bosom, cinched waist, and the curve of my hips. I'd been unclothed for purposes of bathing countless times in my life, but never had I felt more naked. Vulnerable. Assaulted.

Any skepticism I'd entertained regarding the slander visited on his character withered like smoke from a snuffled candle. Nothing short of sudden death would prevent me from releasing his wife from marital imprisonment.

LeBruton said, "Are you certain you aren't in need of a ride, miss? I believe room can be made for you and we'd be happy to escort you home. Wouldn't we, sweetheart?"

The Chinese word for *crisis* combines the symbols for both risk and opportunity. It sickened me that the risk I was about to take endangered Penelope, not me, but there was no help for it.

"I have my own buggy, thank you," I said, "but as you are such a connoisseur of horseflesh, may I be so bold to ask if you'd take a look at my Morgan and appraise his worth?"

The driver grunted. Under his breath, he said, "You're askin' *him* 'stead of me?"

LeBruton crooned, "I'd be delighted to be of assistance, Miss . . ."

"Sawyer."

He introduced himself and his wife, then folded bodily to exit the wagonette. Over his bowed back, I telegraphed to Penelope a visual promise that her secret was safe with me. I believe she nodded in comprehension, but she was trembling so incessantly, I couldn't be sure.

LeBruton took my arm for the brief stroll to the buggy. His fingertips kneaded my skin and underlying muscle in a manner I supposed was intended to reduce me to a quivering mass of unbridled lust.

Once beyond earshot, I interrupted his soliloquy on my beauty and grace to say, "I cozened you away from your rig under false pretenses."

"Oh?" Lasciviousness glowed in his hazel eyes. "And what might those entail, Miss Sawyer?"

"I am an employee of Sawyer Investigations, Mr. Le-Bruton. The agency has been contracted to look into the recent rash of home burglaries."

Damned if the scoundrel's interest didn't flourish with the admission. "Beauty and derring-do? How marvelously exotic."

I went on, "Last night, upon discovering the murder of Belinda Abercrombie, the manservant stopped a buggy drawn by a team identical to yours. No doubt you'll agree, paired palominos are not common."

LeBruton stiffened. His hand slid from my arm. "Mine are stabled at Orman's livery. I wouldn't condone it, but quite possibly Thaddeus hires them out on occasion."

"Do you own the wagonette?"

"No."

"Do you own a buggy?"

"No."

"Then you rent whatever conveyance is required, depending on circumstances."

A shrug served as his response.

"How shrewd, Mr. LeBruton. Letting, rather than owning, gives the impression of a fleet at your disposal, doesn't it? You can avail yourself of a buckboard for a trot around the park, a cabriolet for the theater, and, on somber occasions such as today, hire a wagonette and driver.

"I shan't think the arrangement is terribly convenient for your wife, though, is it? Silly to walk to the livery, to hire a rig for the day. How would she know beforehand if any were available to let?"

Had Penelope ever tried, I was certain Orman was paid to tell her all were hired out. At any given time, it might even be true. Though I might be giving LeBruton more credit than he deserved, it followed that rail agents had been similarly bribed—perhaps warned that Penelope's mind was dangerously unsound.

Hostility replaced every nuance of LeBruton's joie de vivre. "I bid you good day, miss."

"As you wish. I assume you'd rather answer a constable's questions than mine. Of course, there's also the matter of the woman accompanying you last night being a brunette, not a spun-gold blonde."

LeBruton whirled around. "What is it you want?"

"Confirmation that you and a female companion were hailed by Abercrombies' manservant, then you reported the murder to the police."

He bulled up, his lips pressed tightly closed.

"Did you or did you not make the report?"

No response.

"Fine. You give me no choice but to ask your wife if you were home all last evening."

"Go ahead. Penelope says what I tell her to say."

My laugh was as bitter as gall. "Thank you, Mr. LeBruton. That's precisely the reaction I was after."

His eyes narrowed. "What do you mean?"

"Word to the wise, sir. Liars always volunteer more information than necessary. In the future, I'd limit mine to *yes* and *no*, if I were you."

As he stalked off, I begged Papa to watch over Penelope, like the angel I believed him to be.

I looked to the gravediggers shoveling dirt into Belinda's eternal resting place. The nameless constable and the woman I thought to be Gertrude Hiss were nowhere to be seen.

Hell to breakfast, I fumed. I couldn't buggy to the station house and name LeBruton as the driver Jules had hailed. An ensuing official interview would anger LeBruton, who'd then vent his temper on his wife.

Wait and see. My two least favorite activities. If Jules was arrested, I'd intervene. And there were ways of finding out what Gertrude Hiss told the constable I sicced on her. What they might be, I hadn't a clue, but if I set my mind to it, I'd think of something.

NINE

With blurry eyes, I read the passage in the law book again, then a third time. At that, it took a moment to register that my wild-hared hunch was correct.

"Won Li?" I called. "Come here on the double. I want to show you something."

Placing my hands at the small of my back, I stretched, hearing pops and crackles uncustomary for one of my youth and vigor. Pain shot outward across my shoulders and up my neck. Another hour in the Windsor chair and I'd have been crippled for life.

Supper was delicious, plentiful, and a distant memory. The bowl of poppy seed cookies on the table was now as empty as my stomach. I didn't recall eating nary a one.

"Won Li?"

From the kitchen, a surly voice answered, "I am coming."

Which turned out to be when he was darned good and ready, which coincided with the expiration of my patience.

Won Li strolled into the parlor. On the tray he carried were squares of cheese, crackers, and glasses of whiskey and water. I thanked him for the snack, eyed the whiskey with undisguised interest, but took the glass of water.

"What did you want to show me?" he said. "Other than how an excessively loud voice is extremely unpleasant to the ear."

I pointed to a numbered statute. "Read this."

He leaned closer to the page I indicated and squinted to bring the text into better focus. "Yes. That is interesting." Whiskey in hand, he started back to the kitchen.

"Did you even read it?"

He turned and recited the paragraph verbatim.

My patron was an incurable grandstander. I swept the hair back from my face. "Eidetic recall has its advantages, Won Li, but the importance to Penelope LeBruton lies in what the law *doesn't* say."

"What is not specified cannot be enforced."

"Precisely."

He frowned. "It is absurd to try and assemble a puzzle to which you hold the pieces."

"Humor me, please? Just read it one more time."

The ceiling, not the book, was the target of his obsidian gaze as he sipped his nightly jigger of tanglefoot. Why follow instructions to the letter—so to speak—if one can review sentences committed to memory while irrigating one's tonsils simultaneously.

"I still do not approve of your working for J. Fulton Shulteis," he said. "But what you propose is an ingenious method of complying with the law while circumventing it."

I grinned. "Yes, it is, isn't it?"

The statute concerning printed notices of a marital dissolution allowed that they must be published in a newspaper of general circulation and accessibility. It did not stipulate that the announcement, or the newspaper in which it appeared, must be in English.

Won Li warned, "Yet there is no guarantee the outcome will be as you desire. If gossip were edible, few would ever retire to their beds malnourished."

"I realize it's possible Rendal LeBruton could learn of the notice." I grimaced. "It's his wife who'll suffer the consequences if he does." Looking up, I added, "And you, if LeBruton finds out who wrote it."

"The Chinese newspaper editor is the cousin of the sister-in-law of my friend Cheng Xinnong. If asked, he will keep a confidence."

The rush of triumph I'd felt dissolved like mercury in nitric acid. 'Tis the simplest breeze that feeds the gale, said . . . well, someone far wiser and prescient than an orphan from the wilds of northwest Arkansas.

I stood and closed the law book. "You've told me never to overestimate a friend or underestimate an enemy, Won Li. A man who beats his wife won't hesitate a nonce to beat information out of a newspaper editor."

I laid a hand on his narrow shoulder. "Truth is, if LeBruton guesses, or is told of my involvement, he'll know in an instant who conspired with me. I can't—I *won't*—put you in danger."

He laughed, which startled me, as the sound resembled the death throes of strangulation and was heard on the rarest of occasions. "You experiment with gunpowder and homemade nitroglycerin. You build pipe cannons in the toolshed. You concoct deadly gases, poisons, and tinctures like other women divine a new mint sauce for roast lamb, but you shy from endangering me to a mere and mortal bully with a penchant for violence?"

He set his glass on the table and slumped in an adjacent chair, chortling and gasping for breath. The liquor he'd consumed was surely the cause of this singular episode of uncustomary mirth.

At long last, a handkerchief was produced to wick the moisture from his eyes and his pink-flushed brow. He coughed to clear his throat, then reopened the book. Thumbing through its pages, he said, "Please fetch a goodly supply of paper, a pen, and bottle of ink."

I knuckled my hips. "I won't let you do this."

"It is not a question of let, Joby. The decision is mine to make and act upon."

His posture and tone defied argument. Holding a match to every scrap of foolscap in the house and booby-trapping all our writing implements would only delay the notice's translation into Chinese. Every word of it was already graven in his bottomless cerebral cortex.

Morning provided another topic for discussion with my beloved and infinitely aggravating patron. Actually, the debate to-ing and fro-ing over plates of fried eggs, toasted bread, and sliced melon wasn't worthy of clashing tempers, but the angelica oil bath I'd taken the night before hadn't yielded a restful sleep.

Won Li insisted on depositing me at the drugstore to meet with Abelia, the LeBrutons' maid, then driving himself to the newspaper's shanty in Hop Alley. My counter-plan was to leave him at his destination, keep the buggy for my convenience, then reconvene with him at the agency. It was a smart walk from the alleyway between Wazee and Blake to Champa and H, but Won Li's stride wouldn't be encumbered by a chemise, corset, cotton drawers, two petticoats, and suede boots cobbled for style rather than perambulation.

We'd compromised. Ribbon-tied scroll in hand, he was by now likely exchanging pleasantries with the newspaper editor. I halted the buggy as near the door of Cheesman's as I was able.

Taking the precaution of bringing along the market basket, my step faltered at a newsbutcher's spiel. Holding a copy of the morning *Rocky Mountain News* aloft, he cried, "Extra, extra. Ladykiller Thief arrested by police. Read all about it."

I laid two pennies in the butcher's hand and took a newspaper from the stack beside him. Under the banner headline were a series of subheadings set off with ornamental symbols known in the trade as dingbats. "Justice Prevails over Fiendish Atrocity." "Mayor Congratulates Police on Swift Capture." " 'I Am Innocent,' Suspect Proclaims."

My eyes raced down the page, plucking facts from the report's verbose chaff. The suspect, Vittorio Ciccone, had been arrested while attempting to pawn a diamond-and-ruby bar-pin owned by the deceased, Belinda Abercrombie.

The suspicious pawnbroker compared the pin to the illustrated list of stolen jewelry the police had provided every pawnshop, secondhand store, and jeweler in the city, in anticipation of just such an occurrence.

Vittorio Ciccone professed no knowledge of how the piece of jewelry found its way into his pocket, but he admitted hunger had taken precedence over honesty once it had been discovered. He'd ventured into the pawnshop with the intent to sell the pin for the price of a decent meal and hotel room for the night.

I folded the newspaper into my market basket to reread

at my leisure. Ciccone's story reminded me of lies I'd told before practice begat proficiency.

Shortly before Won Li joined the household, an indoor swordfight with an imaginary band of pirates had toppled a kerosene lamp. Flames devoured the roof and one wall of our cabin before I extinguished them with a wet blanket. With Papa due home any minute, I smashed bunches of pokeberries upside my head, letting the crimson juice drizzle down my face and clothing. Wild-eyed with hysteria, I told him Indians had torched the cabin and tried to scalp me, but thanks be to Jesus, I'd escaped into the woods.

His response forced me to sleep on my stomach for a week and eat meals off the charred mantelpiece.

"Live and learn," I said, stepping into the dim coolness of Cheesman's Drug Store. I patronized the tidy dispensary with some frequency, but I still reveled in the laced aromas of perfumes, astringents, French milled soaps, and plasters whose boxes promised the annihilation of more types of pain than a human should suffer in three lifetimes.

Shelved cabinets purveying patent medicines, female remedies, and nostrums of all kind and description stretched from plank floor to ceiling. On the counters were curved glass showcases replete with merchandise to catch the eye and fancy, and the far wall behind the woodstove displayed ready-to-frame art prints of landscapes, flora, fauna, and dead but unforgotten heroes.

I smiled and greeted a bevy of bona fide customers before spying Abelia in a back corner stocked with bath salts and aromatic candles.

"You're late. I'd 'bout give up on you, girl."

Her face shone with nervous perspiration. I saw no

reason to belabor my exacting punctuality. I asked after her mistress and was relieved to hear Penelope was to attend a banquet with her husband later that evening.

"Just goes to show, you don't know beans from applebutter," Abelia said. "That man's as mean as a scalded cat when he's sober, but put the drink in him and he's spoiling for a fight. Miss Penelope'll be in worse shape than you saw her, come mornin'."

"Not if we can prevent it." I told Abelia about the notice Won Li was placing, then said, "In the buggy, I have a jar of castor oil distillate for you. I brought it to impede Mr. LeBruton's daily activities, to lessen the odds of him finding out about the dissolution.

"I'd planned on him receiving the first dose at supper, but begin as soon as you get home. He won't feel any effect for several hours, but each subsequent one will compound the discomfort."

"How much do I give him?" Abelia asked.

"A quarter teaspoon, every six to eight hours. Stir it into his food, or a cold drink, such as lemonade or milk. Coffee or tea are fine, too, if he takes them with cream."

The maid took on the visage of an elderly, nut brown elf. "What if, purely on accident, I slip him a pinch too much?"

I chuckled. "It won't kill him, if that's what you're hoping. It would likely worsen his stomach cramps, until he refused food and drink altogether."

Abelia grunted. "So, I'm s'posed to keep him sick enough to put him outta commission and well enough to keep poisoning him, regular."

"You're not poisoning him, Abelia. Only disrupting his digestion."

"Hush, girl. I've dreamed of poisoning that man since

the day he met up with Miss Penelope. Don't you go spoiling my fun."

A casual glance toward the counter met with Mr. Cheesman's hard stare. A young brunette spraying perfumes on her wrist was watching us from the corner of her eye. Abelia's and my whisper campaign had not gone unnoticed.

I asked her to join me outside after she finished her shopping, then loudly chirped my appreciation for recommending the jasmine bath salts over the gardenia.

I also removed a bottle of Dr. Kilmer's Female Regulator and box of worm expeller from shelves as I passed. I felt duty bound to pay a toll for loitering and figured the pharmacist wouldn't truck with a woman cursed by irregularities of the menstrual cycle and a tapeworm.

Hastily wrapping my purchases in brown paper, he offered to charge them and bill me at month's end. Reluctant to remind him of my name, I dipped into my dwindling cash reserves.

I could have kicked my own derriere for wasting money on claptrap I didn't need and would never use.

The retainer from McCoyne and Whitelaw couldn't be added to the agency's ledger until it was earned. By all rights, it was a loan, repayable by equal outlays of my time and effort. To date, I hadn't expended six-bits worth of either.

Abelia followed me outside a few moments later. She fidgeted as I repeated the dosage instructions. "I done heard ya the first time. Just cause I'm colored don't mean I'm deaf, nor stupid."

I retracted my arm as she reached for the jar. "Before I give you this, you have to promise me something."

"What's that?"

"You must tell your mistress you burned her letter to Mr. Shulteis. I can't aid her escape from her husband without her knowledge and consent."

"I already did," Abelia said. "Not an hour after you left t'other day, she called me upstairs. She was standing in front of the lookin' glass, angry as all get-out with herself for not going ahead with the divorce. When she give me another note to take to the attorney, I told her he never got the first one."

My skepticism must have shown, for she spat out, "That's the *truth,* girl." She yanked a folded sheet of stationery from her shopping basket. "Read this, if'n you don't believe me."

Please forgive my cowardice vis-à-vis our conversation of Tuesday instant. My courage shall not fail me, or you, again. Of that, you may rest assured.
                    Penelope A. LeBruton

I smiled and gave her the jar. "If I doubted you, Abelia, it was because I know how much you love and fear for Mrs. LeBruton."

"Lyin's a sin. I don't tell none, 'cept the tiniest little fibs I trust the Almighty will see fit to forgive."

I removed a fountain pen from my reticule and wrote my home address on the back of a calling card. "Tell your mistress to contact me immediately if she needs me for any reason. That includes shelter or safe passage from the city."

Abelia nodded, her lips pressed as flat as vise jaws.

Being in sight of the end to a long and torturous ordeal ignites a terrible sort of irony. Fear segues to blind rage. Helplessness to vengeance. Hope to violent retaliation.

After all the abuses he'd executed with impunity, I knew if Rendal LeBruton raised a hand to his wife again, he wouldn't live to gloat about it.

For that reason, I didn't mention the telegrams I'd sent. Verily, the subject was moot until I received answers and they confirmed my suspicions.

"Before you go," I said, "how can I contact you or Mrs. LeBruton if necessary? The distillate will keep Mr. LeBruton close to home, if not confined to it."

Abelia's face screwed up, both in thought and repugnance at "that man's" potential quarantine. "That's a puzzlement, to be sure."

I turned my back to the dust boiling up from the street. There was no reprieve from the sun heating to a fair sizzle, as it crept toward midday. Passersby shuffled along as if the boardwalk were as inclined as a rising drawbridge. Mother Nature seemed obsessed with contradicting tourist guidebooks extolling Denver City's temperate climate.

A few yards away, the shapely brunette I'd seen at the drugstore's counter was struggling to open a parasol but watching us from beneath her lashes.

"There was a young woman in the store earlier—petite, hair in ringlets, wearing a beige waist and pink skirts? Are you perchance acquainted with her?"

Abelia grunted. "Don't care to be, thank ye kindly. Mary Anna Squires is her name. She's from back East, visiting kinfolk here for the summer. Mostly, she's consorting with 'that man,' if'n you get my meaning."

I did, but asked, "How do you know?"

"It ain't all recipes and rheumatiz complaints what crosses over the back fence. No coincidence that maids hang laundry the same time and day of the week, neither."

It was also true that a married man out for a late night drive with a woman other than his wife would stay to quiet, unpopulated thoroughfares like California Street. It would thrill me to my marrow if LeBruton and his consort were accomplices to the robberies. Unfortunately, he didn't have the stones for it.

An elderly Samaritan won the battle of Miss Squires's umbrella with a flick of his thumb. The next Mrs. LeBruton thanked him, dispensed a haughty sneer at me, then flounced around the corner.

Damnation. Miss Squires was certain to remark on Abelia's and my whispered conversation inside the store and continuance outside.

"Double the dosage," I ordered. "Keep a sharp eye on the back gate. If you see a strip of cloth between the pickets, meet me at the far end of the alleyway as quick as you can."

"But what if—"

"We've tarried too long, as it is. There's no time for what ifs. Just go home and do as I ask." Abelia looked so frightened, I added, "Everything will be all right. I promise."

I trusted the Almighty would see fit to forgive that fib, too.

TEN

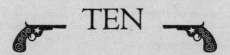

J. Fulton Shulteis was still absent from his office when I returned the law books. Percy expressed his usual delight at my appearance. I asked for his personal guarantee that if Fulton needed to speak with Penelope LeBruton, I would be summoned to act as messenger.

Of his own volition, Izzy turned for one of the Cherry Creek bridges connecting what had been Auraria, Colorado, to its larger sister city. Whether it was simple curiosity or a morbid variety I can't say, but nevertheless I allowed the Morgan to clop to the east side of Front Street, between Larimer and 4th.

The jailhouse there was a bleak, odoriferous facility whose population forever exceeded its bounds by a wide margin. I was of the opinion that if schoolchildren were given tours, any fascination with outlaws portrayed in dime novels would be remedied as soon as they stopped retching.

Won Li argued, if public hangings weren't a deterrent, subjecting youngsters to caged criminals wouldn't be either. The insurmountable flaw was that those who committed crimes did so without the slightest notion of ever getting caught, much less convicted and hanged.

A high counter was manned by a uniformed constable. I asked him to announce my arrival to Jack O'Shaughnessy.

"He isn't here, ma'am. He's never here, lest he's bringing in prisoners. The station house on Holliday is where you'll likely find him."

I was not only already aware of the fact, I'd counted on it. A kicked puppy had nothing on me for heartbreak when I wailed, "What'll I do now? He said before I could see Vittorio Ciccone, he had to be here to authorize it."

Slumping against the counter, head in hand, I blubbered, "I shouldn't have left Mother at all, sick as she is. I can't take time to go all the way to the station house, then back here. I just *can't.*"

"There, there, miss. Don't cry. You don't need O'Shaughnessy's say-so."

"I-I don't?"

"Land sakes, no. I can take you to the cell block." He sucked his teeth. "That is, if you're sure you want to go back there. It's no place for a lady, ma'am."

"A moment to pray for the prisoner's immortal soul is all I ask."

The constable lifted a capacious ring of keys from a wall hook. "No disrespect meant, but I don't think a month's worth of praying would save Ciccone from the lake of fire."

The steel door he unlocked howled open on riveted hasps, then clanged shut behind us. The stench of vomit, human waste, filth, and tobacco smoke was as palpable as fog. Arms reached through the bars, undulating like tentacles. Voices chorused in barbaric disharmony.

His nightstick swinging and connecting with vulnerable flesh and bone more often than not, the constable blazed safe passage down the slimy corridor. He bellowed the prisoner's name. In the cell second to the end, a swarthy man leapt down from a bare bunk suspended by chains. The six others with whom he shared a water closet–sized space leered at me but kept their distance.

Privacy was impossible, yet I asked the constable to afford me some. With trepidation, he said, "Pray fast, ma'am. A couple of minutes is all I'll give you." He retreated to the metal door, the nightstick slapping his palm. The sound broadcast a dare and a promise.

Vittorio Ciccone was in his late twenties and shorter than I, though as lithe and well-muscled as a circus performer. He might be handsome if lye soap and scrub brush were applied with equal vigor.

In tortured English, he asked why I'd want to pray for him. I told him God looked disfavorably upon thieves and murderers.

"I din't kill nobody. Never! I try to sell the pin, yes. I din't steal it." He turned out his left trousers pocket— empty, save grit. "It was here. How, I dunno. I *swear* to it."

"Don't shout at me."

"Sorry. I so very sorry. Please, oh, pretty lady. You got to help me."

"If you're innocent, the court will find in your favor."

"No, no." He shook his head vehemently. "I doan know nobody here. Nobody want to help me."

"How long have you been in the city?"

He shrugged. "T'ree, mebbe four days. I ride the boxcar. I look for work. No money I got for food. Nobody give me work."

Every prisoner in the cell block would wail a similar sob story and proclaim it gospel. Nothing was ever their fault. Always someone else's—always some*thing* else.

"Miss?" The constable tapped the door with his stick. "Time's up."

"Good-bye, Mr. Ciccone."

"No! Lissen to me. Please. You gotta believe." His screams followed me out the door. "The man, he say I send the package. He *lies*. What use I got for mail?"

Other prisoners chimed in, shouting and shaking the bars.

Ciccone yelled, "I canna read. I canna write. I swear, I din't kill no—"

The door slammed, muffling the noise without stanching it. Keys jangled as the constable relocked the door. "That's a nice thing you tried to do, miss, but it's wasted on the likes of him."

The so-called Ladykiller Thief had been a disappointment. Then again, human monsters usually were. To my knowledge, the lone exception was a hulking nightmare known as Phil the Cannibal, who allegedly devoured a couple of Indians and a Frenchman when he ran out of grub during the gold rush.

I asked, "What is this package he's yelling about?"

The constable hesitated. "The postmaster says Ciccone mailed a parcel yesterday. Remembers joking with him about sending a brick General Delivery, but can't recollect who it was mailed to, or where."

"Do you think it was the jewelry from all three robberies?"

"Yep. The loot same as stamped Murderer on Ciccone's

forehead. The trinket he saved out to pawn would have bought train fare to nary anywhere in the U.S. of A."

I wondered how many times Ciccone had executed that deviously simple modus operandi. That he wouldn't again was scant comfort. Cunning, he was. Unique, he was not.

"Has the trial date been set?"

"Week from today." The constable peered out on the street. "There's been rumors of a lynch mob, but I haven't seen sign of one." Walking back to his post, he added, "Can't never tell, though. Folks are plenty riled about him strangling a woman with child. They're saying a noose around that dago's neck'd square things a tad."

I tapped my cheek with a forefinger. "If he's guilty, it would, but I heard the police were questioning Gertrude Hiss and Sam Merck—the Abercrombies' cook and gardener."

His grin was indulgent. "You must keep your ear right close to the ground, ma'am. Those two were rounded up, but nothin' came of it. Ciccone done it, sure as the moon is round."

"Ah, but it isn't a perfect sphere—"

Clattering chains and the thunder of approaching boot steps halted in midstride. I knew before I turned that Jack O'Shaughnessy was standing behind me. The prisoner beside him wore a charcoal gray suit, a crimson vest, and a bloodstained bandage around his head.

Jack motioned me out the door. "Wait for me by the buggy."

"I just—"

"I *said,* wait for me by the buggy."

I cared not at all for his tone or attitude, which I told him when he stormed back out.

"Is that right?" He removed his hat, slapped it against

his trousers leg, then resettled it. "Well, I don't care much for you using my name to dupe a turnkey, so's you can shoot the breeze with a murderer like he's your long-lost cousin Bob."

"I acted on impulse. Curiosity got the better of me."

Jack chuffed. "If that's all you've got to say for yourself, maybe you ought to go back and parlay with Ciccone some more. Till a second ago, I thought he was the worst one for excuses I'd ever heard."

"You're angry. I understand that, but there's no need to be insulting." I climbed into the buggy, pushing away the hand he offered in assistance.

"There is, if it'll get through that ironclad skull of yours."

"Oh, it has, Jack. Dunce that I am, it took a while for it to register. You're always right. I'm always wrong."

"From where I stand, it's the other way—"

Anger had me shaking so hard, my voice trembled. "You don't want an explanation. Wouldn't listen if I tried. All you want is for me to beg forgiveness. To promise I'll mend the error of my ways."

"Uh-uh. Far be it for me to ask for a miracle." Jack planted a foot on the brace. "All I want is one day—one measly, goddamned day—without you pulling some shenanigan or another. That'd be a flat-out wonder to behold."

Shenanigan? Did he honestly believe investigation was just a game to me? Something more exciting than stitching samplers or collecting recipes to bide excessive time on my hands?

A hollow sensation gored my belly. My heart teetered, then skidded into the breach. Ramparts rose and hardened around it, like a protective, defensive cocoon.

"If that's how you feel," I said, "then I see no need to continue being the burr under your saddle."

Jack reared back. "What do you mean by that?"

"Plenty of women would be happy to cook, clean, and wait by the door for you to come through it." The reins slapped Izzy's rump. "I am not, and never will be, among them."

For once, I didn't mind the wind tugging at my hairpins. With the jailhouse stink permeating my clothes, Methuselah's parlor rug didn't need an airing as much as I did. And any oncoming drivers who noticed tears seeping from my eyes would fault the silty breeze.

Towns with fifty thousand or more residents enjoyed the luxury of letter carriers consigned to free mail delivery. Denver City hadn't reached that benchmark as yet, so residents' daily activities included Monday through Saturday jaunts to the post office to collect their mail.

As is true elsewhere, the town postmaster acquired his title by political patronage, not by aptitude or a winning personality. In return for better-than-average pay, he tithed one or two percent of his salary to his political party, plus a five-dollar donation to every state and local election.

The harried jake on the business side of the counter was missing an arm below the elbow and a leg below the knee. A veteran of the War Between the States, I surmised. A large number of Yanks and Rebs had migrated west after Lee's surrender. In search of what, they likely couldn't say, but hoped they'd recognize if they found it.

Papa was of the opinion that war survivors should be counted among its casualties, as no one emerged unscathed from the battlefield. Too often, the most grievous wounds and scars weren't visible on the outside.

"Be with you directly," the postmaster said. "Gotta get this bin slotted afore the train from Des Moines pulls into the depot. They'll be mailbags galore on it, 'les some kindhearted outlaw heisted the car 'twixt here and there."

Law, I was dizzy just watching him deal letters and small parcels from a shallow wooden flat into their respective boxes.

While he worked and I waited, customers streamed in and out the doors—every one of them inquiring if mail had arrived in his or her name. "If it ain't in your box, it ain't come, yet," he answered, his tone sharpening like a stropped razor with each repetition.

A gent about my age blamed the postmaster for another day's passage without a letter from his sweetheart. An older man insisted it was the postmaster's job to cart a package as big as a sofa to his place of business. A mother trailing an offspring like a game of Snap The Whip burst into tears when her box didn't contain an expected money order from her children's father.

"How do you expect me to feed my young 'uns?" she wailed. "I *know* my husband done sent it. I've half a mind to jump back there and turn out your pockets to see what falls out."

The ingress and insults were heavier than normal, but the post office was seldom empty. To hear the grousers talk, you'd think the postmaster was the cause of overdue bills, postage-due letters, stagecoach and train holdups, and every other pet peeve that befell the multitudes. Into the ballyhoo calling him a thief, a cripple and a liar, the postmaster cursed, wrenched off his apron, and tossed it on the counter. His peg leg thumped on the puncheon floor. "Off with you," he said, shooing his detractors to the door. "I'm locking up for the noon hour." His wave included me.

"But all I need is five stamps," I lied.

He exhaled a mighty sigh as he shot the bolt home. Limping back behind the counter, he muttered something about never thinking of quitting his job, other than Mondays through Saturdays.

"Honestly, I can't imagine how you match thousands of names to box numbers, much less remember who sent what parcel when."

He scooped the coins I placed on the counter into his palm. "Beg pardon?"

"My goodness, there's no need to be humble," I said with a teasing laugh. "Why if it wasn't for you, that jewel thief would have gotten away scot-free." Slipping the stamps he tendered into my reticule, I added, "Though I suppose addressing the package for him must have aided your recollection."

"No-o-o. 'Twas already made out to General Delivery when he brung it."

"I see. Well, that explains why the destination remains a mystery, doesn't it? *Had* you addressed it, a man blessed with your powers of recall would remember that detail, now wouldn't you?"

His nod was wary. "Prob'ly."

"Forgive me. I know you're eager to rest and have your dinner, but I've never been this close to a bona fide hero before. The police must have been ecstatic when you told them about the package and described the man who sent it."

The postmaster averted his eyes to a basket of incoming mail. He thumbed through the envelopes, as though counting them, then drawled, "They brung him to me."

I leaned forward, my head angled to one side. "Sorry, I didn't quite hear you."

"The constables, they brought the feller here. Took him to the depot first. Told the agent, same as they did me, that seeing as how the stolen jewels were nowhere to be found, they figured he'd posted them out of the city."

I gasped. "Goodness sakes alive. Was the brute in shackles and leg-irons?"

"Oh, yes, ma'am. The cops weren't taking any chances on that greaser getting loose."

"Greaser?" The derogatory term for Mexican was commonly heard, but not common to my vocabulary. "Vittorio Ciccone is Italian."

"Don't care what the breed is. If they aren't white, they don't belong here. I say, ship 'em all back where they came from."

His spew was all the more chilling for its matter-of-fact delivery. Those I'd heard voice similar opinions with podium-pounding fervor triggered contempt, but not revulsion.

I moved to the door, pausing for him to unlock it. A notice-board on the near wall was shingled in church social announcements, wanted posters, and handbills of myriad sizes, descriptions, and misspellings. Almost obscured by a half-sheet advertising Christmas sleigh-rides was a bold-printed reward offered for information regarding ". . . any and all jewelry purloined from the households of Garret McCoyne and/or Avery Whitelaw."

Tapping the notice with my forefinger, I inquired, "Was this posted before or after Ciccone's arrest?"

"Bef—" The postmaster swung open the door. "Good day, ma'am."

Won Li's fork pecked the rim of my plate. "Eat your vegetables."

I grimaced but speared a chunk of steamed carrot. The nameless dish he'd prepared for supper was a palette of colorful vegetables, pineapple, and melon on a bed of rice, drizzled with fresh lemon. The light, delicious fare piled like cairn rocks in my stomach.

"You are not yourself tonight, Joby."

I sighed. "I've had worse days, but there was nothing about this one to recommend it."

He removed our plates from the table. His empty one went into the granite dishpan. Mine was scraped into a small crockery bowl to be reborn as soup tomorrow evening.

"Sending those telegrams was a waste of money." I picked at a small hole in the tablecloth. "Even if we had it to spare, I should have demanded an advance from J. Fulton Shulteis."

"Did you know you would be sending them when he hired you?"

I shook my head.

"Then it is not spilled milk you are crying over. It is milk from a cow you did not own two days ago."

I gave him a look as nasty as the headache beginning to throb at my temple. "Consistent with the barnyard metaphors, it's also failing to acquire a second basket in which to put Penelope LeBruton's eggs that worries me."

He dried his hands on a sack-towel. "There are several responses as yet to be received?"

"Yes, but . . ." Call it optimism or pragmatism, whenever Won Li's supply dwarfed mine, it knocked the stuffing out of an excellent tale of woe. "I was so *certain* Penelope wasn't the first lonely heart he'd bamboozled. She's accustomed to being catered to, but she's afraid, not stupid. More afraid of what Rendal will do if she tries to escape and fails than of enduring whatever fate dictates if she stays."

"Stick fast to the devil she knows," Won Li said. "A common misconception."

"Especially when, from what Abelia told me, Penelope's father treated her like chattel, too."

The water Won Li poured from the kettle into the dishpan would have scalded the hair off a hog. In winter, he walked barefoot in the snow for miles. *Chi,* he called it. Papa said it was plumb unnatural but wished he had a spot of it.

My forehead beaded just watching the steam billow around Won Li. Wadding my hair into a mussy bun, I said, "When LeBruton courted Penelope, charm couldn't have been enough to gain acceptance in her social circle. He had to appear to be a financial equal. Trouble is, even the appearance of wealth isn't cheap."

Won Li agreed. "The proceeds from one victim, he invested in capturing the trust and love of the next."

"That was my supposition." Hair falling to my shoulders, I stood and rolled up my sleeves to help with the dishes. There weren't many. My patron was as frugal with pots and pans as he was with supper ingredients.

He clucked his tongue. "It is sad to think your Casanova won and wed every woman he romanced."

"Oh, I wouldn't go that far. What attracts a woman to a man and vice versa is too subjective to define, much less anticipate. For that reason alone, some of LeBruton's advances must have been rebuffed by their objects."

"You are certain of that."

"Absolutely."

"As certain as you are that *all* the telegrams you sent constitute a waste of money?"

Two precepts applied to Won Li's brand of logic. It flouted the geometric principle that the closest distance between two points was a straight line, and it was virtually infallible.

Had a railroad spike not been inserting itself a fraction above my cheekbone, I'd have foreseen the intellectual trap he was laying. I'd also have laughed and thanked him for balancing my perspective.

Nodding an acknowledgment exacted enough punishment. I fished the tableware and utensils from the rinsepan, placed them on a towel to drain, then walked as though needles spiked the path to the davenport.

Outside the window, crickets and birdsong pierced the quietude. A vile taste spilled from my throat into my mouth. I covered my eyes with my forearm against the blinding twilight. Cephalalgia wasn't a chronic affliction, but if given a choice, I'd sooner be shot in the head than suffer a bout of it.

The chair Won Li carefully moved alongside the sofa thumped and creaked like a lumber wagon. With the utmost gentleness, he laid a cool, wet towel across my brow.

The Chinese believe when they die, God reaches down and pulls them to heaven by their pigtails. The ultimate punishment one can exact is to cut off a Chinaman's transport to paradise. Though I'd never scoff at or scorn Won Li's religious convictions, I believed just as strenuously, if heaven existed, his ascension was assured, irrespective of hairstyle.

Lifting my hand from the cushion, his thumb and index finger encircled my wrist. The gentle, languid massage gradually descended to each fine bone and knuckle and corresponding aspects of my palm.

As my breathing slowed, the agony at my temple receded but stubbornly refused to wave the proverbial white flag. I knew if a muscle twitched, it would drive the spike deeper.

Won Li's attentions moved to the weblike purlicue between my thumb and forefinger. He applied pressure in increasing increments, as though my hand were a bull's nose, and his fingertips, a brass ring.

A white-hot flash of pain seared my head. As it waned, the throbbing, nauseating, sensory torture melted away. Fear of a relapse held me still and mute for several minutes. Won Li's technique had never backfired, but anyone who'd ever experienced such a malady was loath to tempt fate.

"Better?" he asked.

I peeked from under the towel and smiled at him. "Bliss. Thank you, Won Li."

"Rest then, while I brew a pot of strong, black coffee."

I nodded. The stimulant was a necessary final element of the treatment. Then as soon as he entered the kitchen, I rallied myself into a sitting position. The only side effect of his sorcery was a mild physical and mental lethargy. Had I reclosed my eyes, I'd have fallen asleep in seconds.

A slight tingle remained where Won Li had employed his miraculous curative. Who would guess that pinching the hand a certain way would affect a completely different area of the body? Let alone that the line between pain relief and pain infliction was a miniscule increase in pressure?

Tracing the site on my own hand, I thought back to the bruise on Hubert Abercrombie's on the night of the murder. Laying a finger against the webbed skin, I closed my fist around it, as if climbing a rope.

I supposed that hauling up one's body weight could

contuse the same general area. But if so, wouldn't bruises be present on both hands? My mind was too muzzy to vouchsafe an answer.

The room tilted when I stood, but leveled itself in short order. Won Li was snipping a rose stem to fit a bud vase on the tray he'd prepared for me. And to think I'd accused Penelope LeBruton of being pampered.

The scissor blades snicked shut. He scowled and said, "If I told you to jump from a bridge, you would rush to climb Pike's Peak instead."

"If that's true, I'm becoming too predictable. Next thing, you'll complain about being bored."

"Hah. The meaning of the word is unknown to me."

I bent to sniff the rose's perfume. How sweet it smelled and how wicked its thorns, particularly when blown out a slender, cane pipe.

"Can anemia provoke severe headaches like mine?"

"Yes." Won Li spread my lips apart with his fingers, like a prospective buyer examines a horse. "Your gums are pink, as are your inner eyelids, thus the headaches you suffer are not from thin blood."

I held up my hand. "Hypothetically, if I *were* anemic, would the pressure you applied leave a bruise?"

"It is possible." He pondered a moment. "More possible, I would think, if you were older. The young are resilient. With age comes delicacy and a slowness to heal."

I stared at the *L* formed by my thumb and forefinger. The jailor's voice resounded in my ears. *Folks are plenty riled about him strangling a woman with child. They're saying a noose around that dago's neck'd square things a tad.*

At the time of her death, Belinda Abercrombie was pregnant?

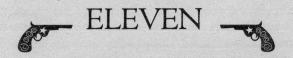

ELEVEN

A train derailment between Golden and Denver City shuttled the Abercrombie murder and Ciccone's arrest off the front page of Friday's edition of the *Rocky Mountain News*.

It had yet to be determined whether a faulty rail or the engineer highballing down a steep slope had sent the locomotive and cars skidding sideward through the trees. A woodcut illustration of the wreckage resembled a giant carpenter's hinged rule smoldering in a pine forest.

The list of dead and injured included no familiar names. I cast the rest of the paper aside, unread.

"What's the matter with me, Papa?" I asked the empty chair across from me. "I can't sit still. I can't concentrate on anything, other than my inability to concentrate. I'd fear I was going stark, raving mad if I thought those who are realize in advance that the mania is upon them."

No phantom voice offered advice or answers. I'd have

welcomed either, but my expectations were as low as my mood. Though I loved my father as fiercely as any daughter could, he'd seldom been within earshot when I'd needed him most.

Kneeling to refold the newspaper, I muttered, "And death hasn't improved your hearing a whit."

Ever since I wakened that morning, a prickly sensation, like a subcutaneous rash, had held hostage my normal serenity and good humor. I'd expected some unease, due to today's publication of the dissolution notice Won Li had translated and placed. I hadn't anticipated the squirmy discomfort common to roosting on a tick-infested log.

There was also, I admitted, a void with Jack O'Shaughnessy's name on it. Our parting was inevitable, I supposed, but I regretted the anger precipitating it.

Except that, too, was inevitable, I thought as I laid the somewhat creased, but current, newspaper on Papa's desk. Just as I triggered the white knight-protector in Jack, the willful child in me was incensed by his criticisms, limitations, and ultimatums.

"Oil and water," I said, lopping off the tip of a fresh cigar. I champed the vile thing between my teeth and struck a lucifer on the lamp base. Applying flame and puffing myself green in the face, I then tamped out the ember in the ash receptacle and coughed my fool head off. Papa simply must quit smoking, or it'd be the death of me.

For strictly medicinal purposes, I took a nip off the pint of Old Cabin. The whiskey blazed a path from my tonsils to my toes, but I didn't choke this time. Albeit reluctantly, I managed to suppress the impulse to test a second swallow for potability in the interest of scientific research.

A wise decision, except it left naught to occupy my mind, or hands, until Won Li arrived in the buggy to fetch me home. The monotonous hours ahead stretched further than the horizon.

Moments later, I set out for J. Fulton Shulteis's office. The mission I'd divined was bona fide, perhaps urgent. At the very least, it would demonstrate Sawyer Investigations' conscientious attention to detail.

My pace was brisk, and my gaze held as level as a debutante correcting her posture by means of a book balanced atop her head. Which isn't to say peripheral vision didn't survey every bay horse, uniformed constable, and broad-shouldered man of taller than average height.

Avoidance was the objective. A recurring tautening at my midsection testified to the fact that all of the above frequented the city streets in droves. I had no acquaintanceship with the O'Shaughnessy imposters, but their sheer number seemed a freak of nature.

While mulling over this anthropological curiosity, I paused before crossing Lawrence Street for two lads and a glossy-coated dog herding a litter of pigs. Blissfully ignorant of what the immediate future held in store, the shoats jogged along, snorting and swiveling their heads like dignitaries at a Fourth of July parade.

In retrospect, sight of Hubert Abercrombie and Garret McCoyne conversing in front of the bank across the street would have escaped notice had the pigs not penned me at the corner.

Their discourse was punctuated by gestures and nods. Abercrombie's pallor was ghostly, even at a distance, but weak blood didn't hinder chuckling at one of McCoyne's remarks.

Oh, how I wished for a thirty-foot-long ear-trumpet to eavesdrop on the parley. They faced each other, so sneaking up for a listen was out of the question. I told myself the topic of discussion could be anything, including the weather. The observation was as effective at tamping my curiosity as spitting on a forest fire.

Starting across Lawrence, I rejected the barbershop west of the bank as a hideaway. The bastion of tonsorial artistry was as forbidden to females as a gentleman's club. To the east was a glover and fur dealer. Just as I conjured an excuse for availing myself of the store's alley entrance so I could peel an ear out the open front door, Avilla strode through it and joined her father and McCoyne.

Other than a dark green dress, she demonstrated no outward indication of unrelieved sorrow. To her credit, I admitted grudgingly. Avilla might have been somewhat fond of her stepmother, but sinking into depression at Belinda's death would be hypocritical. From what Elise had said, the two women tolerated each other. I surmised they might be rivals for Hubert's affection.

By the time I reached Shulteis's office, my imagination had Hubert and Garret McCoyne as coconspirators in the jewelry thefts and murder. Percy's sourpussed expression was a fetid breath of reality.

"Has Fulton returned from Leadville?"

"He has."

"Is he with a client?"

"No, but you don't have an appointment."

I rolled my eyes. "Must we iterate this ridiculous exchange every time I come here?"

"We must, until you extend the courtesy of securing a proper appointment."

"You are nothing if not consistent, Percy." I grinned. "Fortunately, so am I."

The crack of his knee on the drawer coincided with me scuttling into Fulton's office. The attorney's feet were splayed on the desk, and he was sleeping like Father Machebeuf in the confessional.

A sharp rap with an honorary gavel to his shoe sole put an end to that nonsense. Arms aflail like broken wings, Fulton caterwauled remarks denouncing the legitimacy of anyone who'd whack a gout-sufferer's foot with a hammer.

A rap is not a whack and a gavel's shape merely resembles a hammer, but intuition advised against making those distinctions.

Instead, I suggested a medicinal tea brewed from goutwort leaves, nettle juice, and dried self-heal, known botanically as prunella vulgaris. Ingested four to six times per day, it should relieve, if not cure, what ailed him.

The remedy was not one of Won Li's but Dr. Nicholas Culpeper's, an English herbalist, apothecary, and astrologer. Culpeper died from tuberculosis in 1654 at the tender age of thirty-eight. As luck would have it, the disease was one of the few for which he had yet to concoct a treatment.

While Fulton tenderly massaged his foot, I asked whether dear Percy had delivered the message regarding the LeBruton case. The attorney said he had, but he perceived no need to contact Penelope in the foreseeable future. In the interest of brevity, my report on the status of the dissolution neglected mention of the distillate of camphor oil I'd given Abelia. Nor did I dun Fulton for the telegrams. He hadn't authorized the expense, thus I couldn't expect reimbursement.

When I got to the part about publishing the notice in Hop Alley's newspaper, Fulton laughed uproariously. "Brilliant. *Brilliant.* Do tell that ingenious father of yours that I couldn't have circumvented the law any better myself."

My mouth opened, then shut again. Better to bask in the spirit of the compliment than protest the object of it. I asked, "Then there's no question of legality?"

"Not unless Rendal LeBruton raises one."

I tilted my head. "I reviewed your law books thoroughly. There's no stipulation to notices being written in English."

"That isn't the contention." Fulton grimaced as he forced his gout-swollen foot back into a half-boot. "If I represented the respondent, I'd contest that newspaper's abidance with the definition of a publication of general circulation. If a judge agreed, it's immaterial whether it was written in Latin, Greek, and a smattering of Gullah."

My grip tightened on the back of the visitor's chair I stood behind. I'd been so smug about the language oversight I'd disregarded circulation numbers. Common sense said a newspaper legible to a fraction of a county's population didn't meet "general" standards.

"Then we'll simply have to trust that LeBruton doesn't learn of it until the decree is granted."

The attorney tut-tutted. "Which he could appeal, citing the aforestated premise."

Except he wouldn't. Why bother, when LeBruton could bribe his judicial pal to declare Penelope insane and ship her off to the nearest—or farthest—asylum?

Dejection and apprehension tussled for sway as I emigrated from the law office to the LeBruton home. What I expected to find, or accomplish, I had no idea. Signalling Abelia to apprise her of Shulteis's warning would dash hope and reignite desperation.

Other than water dripping from the ferns hanging from the veranda's ceiling, the house looked the same as it had on my first visit—whether peaceful or sinister was a matter of supposition. Like the granny-woman who lived near us in Ft. Smith would say, "You don't judge a church by its steeple."

After being shut up for most of the afternoon, the agency was an oven with furniture when I returned. Bending to stop the door with a brick, I saw a sealed envelope jutting from under the bottom rail. JOBY was hand-lettered on it, in ink. Holding it up to the light merely revealed the dimensions of the note inside.

I tapped the envelope on a thumbnail. "A new client could have left it. Or Abelia. Possibly, McCoyne, or even one of the Abercrombies—a thank-you note, for the cake."

Who was I kidding? I didn't recall seeing his handwriting before, but, "It's from Jack. You know darned well it is."

"It is traditional for mail to be read, not conversed with."

I spun around. Won Li stood in the door, hands clasped in front of him. "Is it not?"

"Then you read it. If it's from Jack O'Shaughnessy, throw it away."

His mouth tucked when I handed him the Arkansas toothpick I used for a letter-opener. Utilizing a Bowie-style knife to slit paper was akin to hunting quail with a cannon, but a woman alone can't be too careful.

Won Li angled his arm, the sheet of stationery suspended over the ash can. "It is an apology."

I needn't ask from whom. To say I wavered would be an understatement. Mutual amends for mutual wrongdoing wouldn't resolve anything, except yesterday's argument. No, in truth, it wouldn't accomplish that, either. Harsh words were but symptoms of the conflict between us. Swapping "I'm sorry's" did not a partnership make, and neither of us would be content with anything less.

I took the paper from Won Li, wadded it in a ball, and dropped it in the receptacle. "Jack and I are too different. Let's leave it at that."

Won Li bowed an agreement, though he didn't, for a scant second. Silent capitulation brooked no hardship for him. He knew I'd contradict myself before the buggy traveled two blocks from the office.

We'd put nearly three behind us when I said, "I was with Jack when he was summoned to the Abercrombie house. I saw that poor woman dead on the floor. I interviewed her husband, stepdaughter, and servants. Is it so unreasonable for me to want to see the man charged with the crime?"

Silence.

"Want to know why *I* think Jack was furious about me visiting Ciccone at the jail?"

Silence.

"*I'll* tell you why. Maybe the mayor, chief of police, and everybody else have convinced themselves that Ciccone is guilty, but I think Jack has his doubts."

I snorted. "*I'm* certainly beginning to. I can't imagine why Jack wouldn't."

Won Li said, "You think very much alike."

"That's right." I pressed two fingers together. "Peas in a pod."

"I see . . ."

"For instance, if Ciccone burglarized the McCoynes, Whitelaws, and Abercrombies, murdering Belinda to make good an escape, why did he mail the spoils, *then* try to pawn a piece for train fare? If he had money for postage, why not spend it on his getaway?"

"Are you certain he paid postage to ship the parcel?"

"Of course, he—" I groaned. "Cash on delivery. Sending it C.O.D. wouldn't have cost him a red cent."

"No," Won Li allowed, "but selling even one item of stolen jewelry in the town in which it was stolen was unwise to the extreme."

I sat up straighter in the seat. "Then you agree? Ciccone may be innocent?"

"If stupidity were proof of innocence, we would have little need for prisons."

"But if Ciccone is as wily and experienced at burglary as one must presume, why was he too penniless to buy himself a train ticket?"

I held up a hand. "And what about this. Why would a young, muscular man strangle a woman with a string of pearls? Why not a forearm to the throat? Assuming he crept up behind her, a quick half-twist to the head would have snapped her spine."

Won Li's lips pulled back, as though he'd swallowed sour milk. "A lady should not entertain such gruesome thoughts."

I chuckled. "Lest you forget, I was wringing chickens' necks for Sunday dinner before you could say 'Arkansas' with all the consonants."

His muttered response was in his native tongue, which I preferred to let him believe I didn't savvy. Truth be told, my grasp was a tick past cuss words, but since he rarely said anything else in Chinese, I didn't miss much.

"So," I pressed, "why did a strong-armed killer use a pearl necklace for a weapon? An *imitation* pearl necklace, I might add. Mrs. Abercrombie owned two real ones but was murdered with the fake."

With his nose stuck high enough in the air to catch flies, Won Li said, "A garrote is silent and efficient. Death comes more quickly than with a choke hold. There is little or no struggle. As life ebbs, the victim claws at the ligature, desperately attempting to loosen or remove it. Hence, he or she does not counterattack the killer."

I shivered. When he put his mind to it, the old Chinaman could out-gruesome me any day of the week. I thought back to the bruised rings at Mrs. Abercrombie's neck; the odd, premortem scratches welting the skin above and below. She must have inflicted them herself, in a panic-stricken effort to breathe, to scream, to survive. Detaching myself from the personal aspect to focus on the psychological, I wondered whether a murderer could rationalize a garrote's swift efficiency as a humane means of death. More so than a knife, say, or fatal blow to the head, since a gunshot was forbidden by virtue of its report.

Methodology take the hindmost. The curiosity that hectored my mind was the means. "Although it's reasonable to surmise that a professional thief could distinguish real pearls from imitations at a glance."

I didn't realize I'd been thinking aloud until Won Li said, "In a book entitled the *Shu King*, written in twenty-three B.C., the author disparages a lesser king for sending a tribute of pearls that were not quite round."

"I thought genuine pearls were always perfectly round."

"You assumed. You did not think." Won Li turned the buggy into the lane, as though Izzy needed guidance to find his way home. "If you had devoted thought, you would know a quirk of nature would not produce perfection, except in the rarest of cases."

I nodded, my eyes wide with comprehension. "Then a strand of perfectly round pearls would expose them as fake."

"Perhaps."

"What do you mean, 'perhaps.' You just said—"

"As always, what I say is not necessarily what you

choose to hear. The gathering of perfect natural pearls in such a number as to string into a necklace is possible, but would be enormously expensive."

"Oh." I sniffed. "You're only arguing for the sake of it. Hubert Abercrombie is quite wealthy."

He slanted me a look. Not another word was said while he unharnessed Izzy, brushed and grained him, and hauled a bucket of water from the outdoor pump. Wed obtuse to obstinate and the result is a slight, sallow-complexioned man named Won Li.

For the one million two hundred and ninety-four thou-sandth time since first we met, my vow not to speak until spoken to went to hell in a handcart when I yelled, "So, how the holy heck do you tell the gosh-danged difference?"

He graced me with that mouth-rumple that sufficed as a smile. "As we have established that although rare, genuine pearls can be as round as artificial ones, other distinctions are evident. They are not noticeable at a glance, however, if the latter are well crafted."

Patience is its own reward, I chanted to myself. Speed is not of the essence. A shut mouth gathers no feet.

"Both should be strung on silk for durability," he said. "A knot is tied between each to prevent their chafing together. The knots also strengthen the silk, but if it should ever break, at most only one pearl might fall off and be lost."

It wasn't surprising that silk won out over cotton thread, or even jeweler's wire. Theories existed that silk fabric could deflect or halt a bullet. To my knowledge, it had yet to be proven, due to a dearth of willing volunteers.

Won Li's lecture continued, "A high-quality artificial

pearl is made by dipping a glass bead in a substance com-
posed of fish scale and lacquer. When finished, the shine
is primarily a surface reflection. The translucence of a
natural pearl glows from within."

Well, that sounded visible to a thief to me . . .

"When viewed in indoor light, the difference in lumi-
nosity is subtle. It is the surface that differs. When rubbed
against the teeth, the natural pearl will feel gritty, whereas
the imitation is smooth and slippery."

Now that he'd mentioned it, I recalled reading about
that common and exquisitely simple test. A second-story
man of any experience would be aware of it, as well. But
would he take the time, minimal though it was, to sort the
bona fides from the fakes at the scene of the crime?

TWELVE

J. H. Hense was a grandfatherly sort with impish eyes. Their light dimmed considerably when I inquired after an elongated-style ring set with turquoise and rose-cut diamonds.

When the item selected from Avery Whitelaw's list failed to materialize, I described Mrs. McCoyne's opal and faceted crystal rondelle bracelet and necklace as a piece my mythical Aunt Ada would also cherish as a birthday gift.

Mr. Hense said he was fresh out of those as well, but perhaps a cameo ringed with pink diamonds would strike her fancy.

"Aunt Ada has several of those," I said. "A pearl necklace might be nice, though I've never noticed her wearing them."

Hense brightened a moment, then was as appalled by what I proposed next, just as his peers—namely, a Mr. Courvoisier and Misters Joslin & Park, all owners of eponymous jewelry stores along Larimer Street—had been earlier.

I'd braved the tidal wave of Saturday shoppers loosed on the city to secure the loan of a strand of genuine pearls and two of the artificial persuasion. By the looks on all four jewelers' faces, you'd have thought the request had been accompanied by a brace of pistols.

"I'm willing to sign a promissory note, a warranty of return—whatever you deem necessary," I said. "Whether my aunt selects a string or not, I'll have the pearls back in your hands within an hour at the latest."

Mr. Hense guffawed, startling an elderly woman browsing a case of watch fobs. "Forgive me, Miss Sawyer. I meant no insult and sincerely hope none was taken, but even if I had a genuine pearl necklace in the store, I wouldn't lend it to my dear, sweet mother for an instant, much less an hour."

I sighed. "Then I suppose I'll have to take three artificial strands on approval. Aunt Ada is so picky, I dare not buy one outright."

His head was wagging before I finished the sentence. "This is a retail shop, not a library. I'll give you a fair price on the necklaces, but that's the best I can do."

My eyebrow cocked. "How much?"

"What length do you prefer?"

Long enough to strangle someone with was the correct answer. I stifled it and hazarded, "Twelve inches."

"Umm, well . . ." Elbow propped on a crossed arm, he hooked a finger on his chin. "Might I point out, as our merchandise is of exceptional quality, the clasps on all our pearls are fourteen-carat gold."

"Lovely. How much?"

"I believe I could let you have them for fifteen dollars.

If the two extras are returned quickly and undamaged, I will refund their purchase price." He smiled. "That is, if your aunt can choose between them."

I sawed my lower lip between my teeth. I could buy two, if I relieved the agency's vault of its paltry holdings. In the manner of a last resort, I said, "No offense, but I don't think five dollars each is much of a bargain."

"Five dollars?" Hense staggered backward, grasping at his chest. "My dear woman, the price I quoted was per each, not the total of all *three*."

Leaving great chunks of pride and the pearls behind, I marched up Larimer toward Roath's, one of the city's five remaining jewelers. Pausing outside the door, I uttered an oath of which Papa was fond, then turned on my heel. Although it's said that a winner never quits, there are more ways to skin a cat than sticking its head in a bootjack and jerking its tail.

The costume pearls I'd seen displayed at Cheesman's Drug Store on Thursday instant were cheap imitations of imitations, but they were bought for two dollars and change—plenty enough to rig a shell game with an accused murderer.

I felt certain my luck was changing when the constable manning the jailhouse's desk was not the one who'd witnessed the discussion between Jack and myself. This officer was twenty years younger and of lanky build. By the gleam in his eye, he was a staunch believer in a uniform's legendary power of seduction.

Because I'm an equally staunch believer in males' fascination with women oblivious to their posturing, I strode up to the counter and said, "How do you do. I'm Miss Alice Peabody, secretary to Stanley Hayden, of the Hayden, Denton and Paxton law firm."

He grinned. Make that leered. "It's a pleasure to make your acquaintance, Miz Peabody."

Presently, I said, "Well, are you going to escort me to the prisoner, or shall I find him myself?"

"Huh? What pris—"

I pointed at the door to an anteroom. "I demand to see your supervisor. He was told to expect me and there's no time to shilly-shally. Our client, Mr. Ciccone, goes on trial Thursday, for heaven's sake."

"Ciccone's got a lawyer?"

"As a matter of fact, he has three. All working pro bono on his behalf." I smirked. "That means at no charge."

Scratching his head, the jailor looked over his shoulder, then back at me. "There's no supervisor on duty, ma'am, but if it's Ciccone you want to see, I'd be happy to take you to him."

"Excellent." I moved to the steel door. When he unlocked it, I said, "As usual, I needn't be accompanied to the cell." A dazzling smile appended a light brushing of his arm with my hand. "If you'd be so kind as to leave the door open? I won't be but a moment."

His return grin was a tad forced. "Best put the hurry to it, then. I'm breaking rules ninety to nothin'.'"

If anything, the stench had worsened, but fewer arms and catcalls greeted my entrance. Ciccone rushed the bars as though I were the resurrection and the light. "Madre de Dio." His grimy hands clapped together. "I knew you would help me, pretty lady."

I held out a pencil and my notebook. "See what's written at the top of the page? Copy it. Please."

"Scuse?"

"I can't help you if you refuse to help me."

Obviously perplexed, his fingers crabbed around the

pencil. He licked the lead, then sketched, rather than wrote, *Vittorio Ciccone. General Delivery. Denver City, Colorado Territory.*

Every *e* was backward, as were both the capital and lowercase *d*'s. The *c*'s and *v*'s were legible, but the end result resembled Egyptian hieroglyphics scripted while blindfolded.

Two millennia ago, Aristotle connected one's style of handwriting to character traits. I wasn't skilled or well practiced at the art, but would one feigning illiteracy be as consistent with errors as with more or less correct letter formation?

Collecting the writing instruments, I then thrust the strands of pearls between the bars. "Tell me, which of these are real and which are fakes."

His eyes narrowed. "How would I to know?"

I yanked them back and turned from the cell.

"Wait! Lemme see, again."

Ciccone looped the necklaces on his open palm. One by one, a finger stroked the beads lengthwise. They were pinched, rolled, prodded, his frown deepening with each action. Backpedaling nearer the miserly window high up on the wall, he rotated his wrist, head angling this way and that.

"The light, it is bad," he said. "I canna be sure."

I clenched my teeth, willing no emotion to show on my face.

Ciccone held out a strand to me. "This one, I think, she is too bright for real. The pearl, it is a soft white, eh?" The other two he ran slowly through his fingers. "Smooth. Ah yes. Very smooth." His full lips bowed into a crafty smile. "These, they are, how you say . . . jan-you-wine."

The necklaces coiled into my outstretched hand, then he curled my fingers into a fist and kissed the tips. "If anything Vittorio knows, it is how to please a woman, eh?"

Had my arm been long enough, I'd have bashed his nose bloody. Instead, I walked away, scrubbing my fingers on my skirt. This time, his bellows were in outrage, not professions of innocence.

The constable insisted on escorting me to the buggy and settling me in it. "I'm off duty tomorrow night. I know it's Sunday and all, but I'd be honored to share a meal with you before evening services." A shoulder hitched. "Or after, if you'd druther."

"How sweet of you to ask, but I'm afraid my fiancé wouldn't approve."

His dejection was evident, but I wagered he wouldn't dine alone on his night off. "Anyhow, it was nice meeting you, Miss Peabody."

"And you, Constable."

Eager to decamp from the calaboose before a particular Irishman happened by, I brought down the reins on Izzy's rump a mite harder than intended. He bridled, then hiked his tail and emitted a raucous burst of organic methane gas.

The stink took away breath I hadn't yet recovered from my foray at the jail. I daren't say so aloud, but the apples Izzy had come to expect were embargoed till further notice.

As for Vittorio Ciccone, I was of two minds. The parcel he allegedly mailed could have been pre-addressed by someone else.

For all his fiddling and fondling, not once had he touched a pearl to his teeth. Yes, he'd identified two fake necklaces as genuine, but I'd sought conclusive evidence. Pass or fail, my silly tests were circumstantial and marginally so, at that.

I was missing something, and not just Jack O' Shaughnessy and the two dollars and change I'd spent on jewelry I'd never wear. There was naught to do but begin at the beginning and pray the truth will out.

Back at the office, the agency's city directory yielded home addresses for Garret McCoyne and Avery Whitelaw. On the plat map affixed to the wall, I traced a line from the former to the latter and on to the Abercrombies. If there was a pattern, other than the net worth of the victims, it was lost on me.

At my return to the buggy within minutes of departing it, Izzy jerked his muzzle from the water trough. Enthusiasm for yet another jaunt about town was relayed by a pair of dolorous, brown eyes.

I found the McCoyne home was surrounded by an imposing fence of wrought iron. Lancets picketing the top lent a medieval effect, whereas the three-story house was an agglomeration of gingerbread, furbelows, turrets, obelisks, and millworked foofaraws painted every color of the rainbow, and then some.

Either the man of the house was nearsighted and colorblind to boot, or Mrs. McCoyne's charms were abundant beyond belief.

I never read, asked, or was told where the thief gained access, though Whitelaw had mentioned a second-story window. Hypothetically slipping my feet into a burglar's soft-soled shoes, I surveyed the neighborhood, then the McCoyne home's calamitous facade.

There were no handy balconies. I wouldn't have trusted the fancy trimwork not to give way during a critical and perhaps injurious stage of my ascent. To shinny from ground to roof by means of a downspout, then lower myself with rope to a window, begged notice by anyone in the vicinity.

The alley side of the house was more pregnable from a covert standpoint, but a climb to the roof and descent to a window was still the safest, quietest means of entry.

The same held true at Avery Whitelaw's home, although his brick abode was as unadorned and boxy as a warehouse. Again, the most surreptitious entrance was from the back of the home, by means of the mansard roof.

Both difficult but hardly impossible for a lithe, well-muscled thief. By comparison, the intrusion through Belinda Abercrombie's bedroom window was less of a challenge than burgling Judge Story's office at the Van Buren courthouse.

Vittorio Ciccone likely possessed the required upper-body strength. His height—or lack thereof—also seemed advantageous, as he'd make a smaller target for observation.

The ease of detecting an object decreases in proportion to its size, which, as Won Li elucidated, is one reason knots are tied in the thread when genuine pearls are strung. If broken and unsecured, the precious gems could easily roll under a piece of furniture and virtually disappear from sight.

With a final look at the exterior scene of the second crime, I sighed and said, "Let's go home, Izzy."

If there was another young woman as exhausted and frustrated as I in all of Denver City, I'd have enjoyed commiserating with her in a peaceful salon, where corset stays loosened with abandon and sweet red wine flowed like water. And there'd be a bushel of chocolate drops, like the ones Papa brought home when he'd leave for a week and stay gone for three.

The vision hoved behind my eyes a moment, only to be supplanted by Ciccone's swarthy face. He was a drifter. A street-tough. A congenital no-account destined for territorial prison or the gallows, but I was gut-certain he wasn't a cat-footed burglar and he hadn't murdered Belinda Abercrombie.

I knew as well as my own name who had and why. All I had to do was prove it. Somehow.

Aloysius Q. Dablemont and his rainmaking machine had already been run out of town: thus the Almighty received full credit from the congregation for Sunday morning's thunderstorm. A daisy it was, too, roaring down off the mountains, hurling lightning bolts, hailstones, and ziggety-zag winds.

The gusts held no candle to the preacher's hosannas, though. He outlasted them by three-quarters of an hour. When the choir shut their songbooks, the gullywasher was just a plain old soaker of a rain.

I was seated on the aisle in a rear pew. The last-in-first-out rule applied, but I tarried in the vestibule. Beyond the open double doors, the splattering rain sounded like a skilletful of hot grease. Folks shook hands with the reverend and chatted as long as they dared, then bowed their backs and dashed out, as though vaulting off the deck of a ship.

A hand clamped my shoulder and spun me half round. Mary Anna Squires whispered, "What have you done with Rendal?"

I blanched. "I haven't done—"

"Don't play coy with me, Miss whoever-you-are. You were cozied up to his maid the other day. The desk clerk says he hasn't seen Rendal since the night before that."

Comprehension was sluggish for one with a reputedly agile mind. Jealousy, more so than concern for LeBruton's well-being, was the crux of the matter. The two-fisted phi-landerer must also have taken a hotel room to foment bachelorhood.

I looked the debutante straight in the eye. "I don't know you. I've never met anyone named Rendal. Why you saw fit to accost me in church, I can't divine, but I'll thank you to leave me be this instant."

The vixen bared her teeth, then tossed her head and flounced away.

I sent up a silent prayer that LeBruton was decommissioned, not deceased. It was followed by thanks for leading me from the temptation to tell Miss Squires to avert her inquiries to Rendal's wife.

Elise Estabrook strolled from the sanctuary, talking to a heavyset woman with a rictus smile. I suppose my eagerness to catch Elise's eye showed, for her companion nodded in my direction.

"Jody," Elise said, "I didn't realize you attend our church." She cackled. "Though why I'd have noticed you, I can't imagine."

"Nor can I," I said, laughing. I sincerely hoped I'd be as blithely outspoken as she when I reached her age.

She introduced me to Maude Blount and her similarly corpulent husband, Terrance, then to Durwin Estabrook, a towering, silver-haired man who walked with a cane.

"Jody is a detective," Elise said to no one in particular and everyone in earshot.

"It's Joby. Short for Josephine Beckwor—"

"Jody is investigating Belinda Abercrombie's murder. Or *was*, anyway." Elise's head tilted sympathetically. "Poor thing. Locking up that dreadful Italian put you out of a job, didn't it?"

I definitely loved this woman. "You mean you haven't

heard? Vittorio Ciccone was released from jail late last night."

"What's that?" Durwin leaned forward on his cane. "You mean the police just turned him out on the street? By jingo, the man's a cold-blooded killer!"

Several of Terrance Blount's chins buckled. "I don't believe it. You must be mistaken, Miss Sawyer. They had him dead to rights."

"Besides," Maude chimed in, "if they had, the news would have been all over town before now."

"My source must remain confidential," I said, "but you might say I heard it straight from the horse's mouth." In truth, Izzy heard it from mine, when I'd rehearsed this monstrous prevarication in the stable at dawn.

"I wonder if Hubert knows yet," Durwin said. "Heaven save the chief of police when he finds out."

Elise agreed. "Maybe we should call on him and Avilla. Better to hear it from us, than one of the servants—or worse, read it in tomorrow's newspaper."

I wrung my hands. "You won't say who told you, will you? It could compromise my informant, if Mr. Abercrombie storms police headquarters . . . not that it'll do any good."

Durwin chuffed. "The devil it won't. Hubert isn't in the best of health, but you'd never guess it when he loses his temper."

"Which he'd have every right to do," I countered, "except everyone on the force from chief to turnkeys has been ordered to deny they've dropped all charges against Ciccone. They hope the real killer will be apprehended before his release becomes common knowledge."

"That I *can* believe," Blount said. "The mayor and the chief have backslapped each other silly since the arrest.

This being an election year, the egg'll be so thick on their faces, they'd never get it scrubbed off."

In a quavering voice, little removed from a shriek, Maude said, "Who cares a whit about politics? There's a lady-killing burglar roaming the streets. What will those fools have to say for themselves if he strikes again?"

"Careful, Maude," Elise warned. "Keep screeching like a scorched cat and they'll draft you into the choir."

"How *dare* you—"

"How dare I what? Use common sense, instead of having a hissy fit in the middle of the vestibule?" Elise scouted her audience and found them attentive, then looked from her husband to the Blounts to me. "Has it occurred to anyone other than myself that the police may have freed this Ciccone person for the express purpose of catching him red-handed?"

A man standing with his back to me pursed his lips. Beside him, another exchanged a speculative glance with a woman I presumed to be his wife.

Durwin said, "If they don't yet have the evidence to convict him, that could be a clever strategy."

"Give him enough rope and let him hang himself," Blount agreed.

To me, Maude said, "I promise I won't mention your name, but I won't keep this a secret from my daughter, daughters-in-law, and close friends. If anything should happen to them . . . well, I simply couldn't live with myself."

Eyes downcast, I nodded as if in resignation.

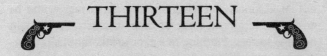

THIRTEEN

Having set countless tongues wagging in trepidation by slandering the mayor, chief of police, and, by default, the entire department, I sallied forth to the LeBruton home. The buggy's hood shielded me head to knees from the slanting drizzle. The balance of my anatomy—most especially my feet—couldn't have been wetter had I waded a creek and sunk to my hocks.

Gloomy befit the house's mien, but any bright spots in Arapahoe County this day were cloistered indoors. I whoaed Izzy at the mouth of the alley.

I swear, ten full minutes must have passed before I gnawed apart a length of lacy ruffle from the hem of my petticoat. The factory's seamstress could not be faulted for shoddy workmanship or cheap thread. After winding the raveled strip round my bent arm like a skein of yarn, a fist-sized knot was then tied at either end.

Due to ruts and pond-wide puddles, my duck-walk to

pass unseen between analogous plank fences was literal, rather than a parody. With the signal rag jammed in a fork in the LeBruton's gate, I returned to the buggy, drenched from head to toe.

Papa told me my birth had been premature by a few weeks. Age had not improved my affection for waiting on much of anything. If I owned the world, trains would run on time, appointments of all kinds would be contracts, not suggestions, and telegrams and signal rags would be answered within an hour of their dispatch. I'd brought nothing to read. Nothing to eat, or drink, though if dehydration seemed imminent, I could always suck a pint or two of rainwater from my sleeve.

With some regularity, I was hailed by passing Good Samaritans who must have assumed I was stranded and didn't have sense enough to walk to the nearest warm, dry house and beckon assistance.

I couldn't convince Izzy that our wretched existence was good practice for the escapade planned for the following night. He fidgeted in his harness and, on occasion, lurched against the breast collar in case I was ready to leave but had neglected to tell him.

A true quandary presented itself at the ninety-minute mark. The need to relieve myself weighed heavily on more than my thoughts. The fear Abelia would scurry down the alley moments after my departure wrestled with suspicion that I might sit there till the snow flew without laying eyes on her.

The prospect of knocking on the front door like a citizen seemed foolhardy. I had no idea what had transpired over the past four days. How would Abelia react to my appearing on the porch? Or Penelope? Or me, if Rendal should answer the bell?

Too late I realized that a second signal, denoting all was well, should have been agreed upon.

"There's no sense in changing clothes just to go back out in the rain."

Won Li said, "Your lips are blue. You are shivering. If you want my help, do as you are told."

"Damned stubborn Chinaman" was the kindest thing I said as I flounced to my bedroom. When I came out, the table was laid with a serving of chicken stew, cold biscuits, and rice pudding.

"Thank you, but I'm not hungry." My stomach growled like a rusty hinge.

"Eat." He pulled out a chair and sat down, hands folded on the table. "Then we will go."

"Now who isn't listening?"

"If a tragedy has occurred, there is no remedy you can provide for it. Regardless of the circumstance, if you become ill from the damp and no nourishment, you will be of no help to Mrs. LeBruton or Abelia."

An hour later, we fussed about who should ply the buggy's reins. My sole objection to Won Li driving was the necessity of changing places before we reached the LeBrutons'. I swear to goodness, I do believe his haggling was founded on the chance of winning an unheard-of three arguments in a row.

He didn't, but twosies were naught to sneeze at.

Izzy's coat and mane had dried, sheltered as he was under the stable's lean-to, but he wasn't eager to get wet again. Although the rain had ceased, not a wink of blue rent the clabbered sky.

I enjoyed using the whip less than he appreciated its sting. He must have perceived I wasn't bluffing, for at the squeak of the handle twisting from the socket, the Morgan stepped lively.

I refrained from driving by the house or down the alleyway. A Robin Hood's barn approach was more discreet, particularly with Won Li riding shotgun. I dropped him at the corner, then continued across the street until I could view the LeBruton front entrance on the diagonal.

As a precaution, Won Li was to offer his services as a gardener first to the LeBrutons' next-door neighbor. Upon reaching the property line, his metamorphosis from dignified Asian gentleman to obsequious servant was astounding.

He was a learned man—a professor of Asian antiquities—until a rival colleague had him shanghaied. Won Li nearly died during the voyage to America in a ship's hold crammed with peasant laborers. Between the rancid food, brackish water, foul air, and stench of never-emptied slop buckets, it's a miracle any of them survived.

In China, Won Li's field of study had made him somewhat of a celebrity. To American employers who'd hired him to lay railroad tracks he was just another Chink. Ironically, his compatriots ostracized him because of his education and higher caste.

From the buggy, I watched Won Li's shoulders round as if a pannier of rocks were strapped on his back. Chin tucked and hands clasped, his sandaled feet scuffled along the brick sidewalk. No one would guess he spoke three languages, had the equivalent of a doctorate in history, and had dined with the emperor at his summer palace.

Shooed away by the neighbor's maid, he continued on to his objective. Nibbling a fingernail, I counted the seconds elapsing after his knock. I pictured Abelia trudging across those polished oak floors, muttering about there being only one of her and she was hurrying as fast as she was able, and if that wasn't fast enough, the visitor could by-gum go hang, for all she cared.

Won Li's arm raised a second time. What if no one answered? No, someone *had* to be home. Yet it wouldn't be beyond the pale for a coolie's summons to be ignored— on a Sunday, or any other day of the week.

Much like yesterday, when you ignored that small voice in your head urging you to ring the damned bell, not just walk on by.

A hand was on the dashboard and my foot was poised above the brace when I saw Won Li's head bob in a subservient manner. Unless it was Rendal standing in the shadows, Won Li was quietly identifying himself and purpose of his visit.

The door's slam startled me and a half-dozen birds roosting in tree branches. Won Li paused, then turned and shuffled from the veranda. He didn't look up at me. I'd asked him not to, but such requests had seldom met with cooperation.

I wheeled the buggy around the block to meet him at the corner opposite where I'd let him off. As planned, he ventured up to the house on the other side of the LeBrutons'. He vanished behind an overgrown boxwood hedge. When he failed to reappear in the span of a rebuff, I searched him out.

I found him talking to and trading arm motions with a bow-legged codger in a tattered robe. The lower half of Won Li's face was obscured by the bell of the old man's ear-horn. I walked back to the buggy, assuming my patron would join me momentarily.

He did not.

When raindrops began to pelt the ground, I assumed it would hasten his return.

It did not.

I was a tick from marching down the sidewalk to remove him bodily before someone—chiefly, a LeBruton or Abelia, if any or all were still alive—called a constable on the demented young woman who'd dithered away the entire afternoon sitting in a buggy, in the rain, conversing with her horse, or more often than not, herself, when Won Li stepped from behind the hedge.

"For the love of Mike, will you *hurry up?*"

He didn't.

God is my witness, he even patted Izzy's neck and praised him for his patience. I plied the reins the instant Won Li's derriere swung into the seat. His landing was a tad off-kilter, but he had the reflexes of a cat. "Please, do ask another favor of me, soon."

"All right, that was mean, but hell and damnation, Won Li. My heart was jumping out of my chest, while you were nattering on with that deaf old man. I couldn't have been more conspicuous if a brass band had marched by."

Silence, then, "Are you finished?"

"Yes."

"The maid answered the LeBrutons' door. I said, 'I'm Won Li,' to which she replied, 'Well, I'm one second from kicking your butt off'n my porch,' then she slammed the door."

"Before you could give her the note."

"That is correct."

"Bullpats."

Won Li cleared his throat. "As for the elderly neighbor,

tomorrow I must borrow the buggy to return and trim the hedge, salt the back walk, and repair loose shingles on the porch, for which I will be paid handsomely."

"*What?*" Izzy veered in startlement. "Have you lost your mind?"

The look I received could have roasted chestnests. "I purported to be a gardener. Mister Ernst is in need of a gardener. Could I have refused?"

"No," I allowed. "The city is alive with gardeners. Mister Ernst won't have any trouble finding someone else."

"Not that he will need to."

"Excuse me?"

Won Li stared straight ahead. "It was I who was hired. It is I who will do the work. I will hear nothing more about it."

"But—"

"Mister Ernst also told me that Penelope LeBruton is abed with female complaints and her husband is plagued by a bilious stomach. 'Sumbitch is wearin' a trench to the outhouse' is how it was put."

I worried a lip. LeBruton's misery was excellent news. I wasn't at all sure whether Penelope had collapsed from the strain, or Rendal had gotten his licks in before his bowels had revolted.

"You have done all you can for today, Joby. Tomorrow, I will be in a position to monitor the LeBruton household."

"I know. That does relieve me some."

He reached to pat my hand. "You have a kind and steadfast heart."

"Why, thank you, Won Li."

"It is only your mind that fails now and then."

* * *

Within twelve hours, I couldn't have agreed more.

Clad in one of Papa's old Union suits dyed a mottled shade of black, I'd been stationed behind a scuppernong arbor since shortly after night had fallen.

The rain chilling me to the bone must have discouraged my suspect. I thought it might, before committing myself to braving the elements, but the chance of guessing wrong was too high to risk.

The windows I'd watched for what seemed like an eternity had been dark for quite some time. No horses' hooves had clopped along the street for an hour—mayhaps longer. A tomcat prowling for love, or a late-night snack, had scared the pee-waddin' out of me, but even the dogs and answering coyotes had retired.

The cloud cover was too thick for a sliver of moonlight to filter through. Scant visibility was as advantageous to me as it was to the faux-burglar who'd murdered Belinda Abercrombie, then rifled her jewelry case, stuffed the plunder in a pillow slip, and escaped without ever setting foot outside the house.

Catching the suspect in the act of framing Vittorio Ciccone for another crime was all that kept me sentried and marginally intoxicated by the pungent aroma of crushed grapes fermenting in the soggy grass.

FOURTEEN

Monday dawned as gloomy and wet as Sunday had ended. Farmers and cattlemen were surely rejoicing an end to the drought, but Denver City's packed-dirt streets had gone from elongated dust bowls to elongated soup bowls.

As a saddle-mount, Izzy was a mudder par excellence. Papa used to brag that his surefooted Morgan could traverse the Arkansas River without bogging a nonce. Unfortunately, slogging a sea of clay gumbo with a buggy at his backside was a different matter entirely.

He was lathered and blowing hard when I deposited Won Li and a satchel of tools at the corner of the LeBrutons' block.

"Don't you dare hazard up on that roof," I warned, "until the rain stops."

"If I loitered until then, what need would there be to repair the damaged shingles?" With that, he tipped his gray felt hat and proceeded down the sidewalk.

Had I not been so eager to get to the office, I'd have dallied to await his flailing, Chinese curse-worded, unstoppable slide. At such time, I'd have rushed to break his fall, which arguably could have proven fatal, thus doubling his indebtedness to me.

That'd teach him.

Within a quarter hour, I sorely wished I was hunkered down in Mr. Ernst's rain-soaked shrubbery as well. Whether a rescue or another bout of the chilblains came of it, either would have been preferable to my encounter with Darius H. Sweet.

The land agent, a second cousin to Beelzebub, earned a living inflating and collecting rents for absentee building owners, plus dunning them for maintenance expenses, bogus taxes, levies and whatever else he could dream up and pocket the money.

He was snugged upside the agency's door, obviously having taken up his post a while ago, with no intention of abandoning it until a Sawyer of some persuasion arrived.

Had Papa been of this world, he'd have scared the water out of Darius Sweet without uttering a single word. I'd proffered numerous requests for an otherworldly haunting of the ferret-faced extortionist. I reckoned that Papa had either ignored them, or Sweet was impervious to vengeful apparitions.

"Are you aware of what day it is, Miss Sawyer?"

"Yes, Mister Sweet. I do believe it's Monday."

Scurrying noises accompanied the creak of the door swinging open. Rats seeking shelter from the rain, no doubt. I looked at Sweet, his dripping hat and overcoat forming puddles on the floor. Present company included.

"It is also the day rents are due, Miss Sawyer."

"I'm aware of that." I scooped up three yellow telegram

envelopes that had been poked through the mail slot. I pressed them to my bosom, as if it would affect their content.

"Then if you'll pay what's owed for office space and your house," Sweet said, "I'll write out a receipt and be on my way."

"I didn't expect you first thing this morning," I said, primping in the reflection from Napoleon's portrait. "Usually you don't collect until later in the afternoon."

"Time of day is no consequence. Either you have the money, or you don't."

I turned and knuckled my hips. "I go to the bank between noon and one o'clock, Mister Sweet. You may stop by again this afternoon, at your convenience."

"Oh, bosh. What you're telling me is that you don't have the money."

"Not in hand, no." I wouldn't have it this afternoon, either, but so far, I hadn't lied once.

"I'll be back, Miss Sawyer. Make no mistake about it."

"Fine. I'll be here when you return." If I was, I'd keep the door bolted and duck behind the desk to evade him. The line between truth and falsehood was often finer than frog's hair.

He paused at the threshold. "There will also be a two dollar-per-rent surcharge assessed for returning a second time."

I nodded. What else could I do?

"And if you're, shall we say, called away before I arrive, an additional five-dollar-per-rent late-fee will be added."

You mealy-mouthed, scum-toothed son of a carpetbagger. Tenants already scraping nickels together can barely hash what's owed, let alone your usurious penalties.

Aloud, I said, "I have business to attend, Mister Sweet."

He sneered. "Oh yes. I can see you're in danger of being trampled by a horde of paying clients."

I made a mental note to ask J. Fulton Shulteis if Sweet's monthly robbery was legal, then ripped open the first telegram's envelope. Scanning the abbreviated lines, I cursed and sailed it into the ash can.

I'd have had the blasted rents if I hadn't put inordinate faith in a hunch. Nor would my skin be as gray-green as moldy bread from my neck to my comely ankles if I hadn't sat in the rain half the night in a baggy, old Union suit. Or had I remembered to add a splotch of vinegar to the dye-bath.

If I owned the world, Mondays would be stricken from the calendar and replaced with another Saturday. Doubtless, the Gregorians didn't know one from the next when they invented it. If they had, they'd have tacked a thirty-first one onto April, June, September, or November, instead of skimping on February's allotment, three years out of four.

The second telegram I skimmed, laid aside, then snatched up and reread. The third message had me screaming "Hallelujah" and running to fetch my hat.

Suffice it to say, my entrance to the police department station house was less than demure. The constable in charge, a sergeant by the name of Nasmith, refused to dispatch a squad of officers until I could explain why I wanted them with some degree of comprehensibility.

Drawn by the commotion, three, then four, constables crowded in to give audience to my explanation. I'd hardly begun relating my theory that an abuser was likely to have engaged in similar acts over a lengthy period of time when Jack O'Shaughnessy strode in the front door.

I hadn't asked for him when I'd arrived, but now said

with infinite sincerity, "Oh, thank God you're here." The sentiment was echoed by Sergeant Nasmith.

"Oh, yeah? Well, I've been looking all over Creation for you. I heard a rumor got started yesterday by a—"

"Never mind that now." I thrust out the telegrams. "Rendal LeBruton, otherwise known as Randall Burton, Burton Randall, and R. Leroy Bruton, is wanted in Sacramento, California, and Comstock, Nevada."

Jack whistled backward through his teeth. "Holy Moses. Bigamy, fraud, attempted murder, suspicion of murder . . ." He shook his head. "Did you know this when you asked me about him at dinner the other night?"

"Of course not. I had my suspicions, but if I'd had any proof, I wouldn't have spent a week absolutely terrified that he'd beat Penelope to death or ship her away to an asylum."

To Sergeant Nasmith, Jack said, "Remember that assault case a few months ago? Name's LeBruton. The lady that went after her husband with a knife and fell down the stairs?"

"Sure do. I was on that call." He chuckled. "Never did figure out why she didn't cut herself to pieces on the way down. Tweren't a speck of blood on her, that I could see."

I growled low in my throat. "Was the knife in her hand or near her when you arrived?"

His mouth pursed. "No, ma'am. Now that you mention it, the husband told us about the knife. I just figgered he'd—"

"You didn't *figger* squat, Nasmith." Jack's baritone ricocheted off the grime-crusted walls. "There's no way in God's green earth a body can fall down a flight of stairs, knife in hand, without cutting themselves somewhere."

Nasmith blustered, "Hold on, there, bub. Best I recollect, you weren't even there. Where do you come off telling me how the cow ate the cabbage?"

"I didn't have to be—"

"She was drunker 'n two barn owls, man. Prob'ly went limp as a rag doll. Her husband said she'd started hitting the bottle . . ." The sergeant's voice trailed away.

"That's right," Jack said. "The husband this, and the husband that." The telegrams rattled like dry leaves. "Miss Sawyer had the smarts to wire California and Nevada and see if there were any warrants on *the husband*. If she hadn't, it's your hands Penelope LeBruton's blood might've been on, by and by."

He pointed to the other constables, who'd backpedaled as far as the wall allowed. "Kent. Paglia. Come with me." To Nasmith, Jack added, "Why don't you think about those cows and cabbages while we're out arresting Mr. LeBruton."

The instant we were outside under the awning, I said, "Thank you for the compliment."

"You deserved it, darlin'. I only wish you'd told me about LeBruton before."

"I should have, I suppose—though after you told me about that earlier call, I wasn't sure what to believe. Then Belinda Abercrombie was murdered and . . ." I smiled. "Well, opportunities got kind of scarce."

"Especially after I went to your office and gave you what-for, then really let 'er rip at the jailhouse." He grinned. "It's enough to make me think I oughta wear my hat on my hind-end, often as it seems to belong there."

Officer Paglia stepped out the door. "Be ready to roll directly, sir. Kent's bringing the paddy wagon around."

"Sooner the better." Jack glanced back at me, then rolled his eyes. "Yes, I was just about to ask if you wanted to follow behind. Like I needed to."

I could have kissed him. Except it would have been in broad daylight on the street and in front of another cop. A lady must have standards and adhere to them. Starting for the buggy, I heard Jack say, "But you're not going into the house with us."

Naturally, I intended to do precisely that. It riled me no end when Jack ordered Constable Kent to guard me at the curb, for crying out loud.

A very wet, mud-caked Won Li scooted into the buggy beside me. He opened his hand to show me the coins he clutched. "An honest day's work for an honest day's pay."

I turned to look at Mr. Ernst's precision-trimmed shrubbery. A square of new shingles contrasted with the weatherworn roof. "An honest day's work, for sure."

"He offered me more. I took as little as he would allow."

I reared back my head. "Why? You must not have taken time to wipe your brow, since I left this morning."

Won Li shrugged. "Mr. Ernst is a man of humble means. I am a man of humble needs. It was a square deal."

Laughing, I hugged his mucky shoulder. "A square deal, eh? Next thing you know, you'll let out a 'yeehaw.' "

"No. I think not."

A fair ballyhoo erupted on the LeBrutons' veranda. My first glimpse of Penelope's husband had him dressed in silk pajamas and shackles on his wrists and ankles. Red-faced and sweating, he struggled mightily to free himself from Jack's and Officer Paglia's grasp.

I could see why Jack had chosen the barrel-chested, neckless Paglia over Constable Kent. The younger, more slender officer would be bouncing off the porch posts and hand railing like a rubber ball.

From the house, a woman screamed, "No, *no.* Don't

take him away. Please, don't. He hasn't done anything wrong."

A second voice yelled, "Get yourself back in here."

A sobbing Penelope LeBruton ran out and launched herself at Jack. "Let him go. Let him go, damn you."

Abelia wailed, "Oh law, Miss Penny. Don't do this. I'm abeggin' you. Come on back in the house with me."

Officer Kent ran to pull the hysterical woman off Jack's back. I swung a leg out of the buggy. Won Li grabbed my arm. "Sit down."

"I can help Abelia calm Penelope down."

"No, you cannot. The maid will take care of her mistress. I am certain she has done so before."

I fell back in the seat. "I don't understand. How can you know that?"

"It is the most vicious of circles, Joby. It is no different than the dog who never knows whether his master will beat him or speak lovingly and stroke his head. He tries his utmost to please his master, thinking if he does enough, is loving enough, the beatings will stop.

"He may dream of running away, of biting the master—killing him, even. After a while, the dog has no will of his own. He comes to believe he deserves the pain. If someone should take the master from him, he will attack the rescuer, for if the master is saved, perhaps the dog will be loved in return."

Abelia and the constable were dragging Penelope back into the house. I thought about Janey Lou Bakker, who'd stayed with and defended her husband until the day he'd killed her. "She's a grown woman, not a dog."

"The analogy was intended not as an insult but as a commoner example. You have never received such treatment, hence it is difficult for you to conceive of it."

Anger, compassion, mystification, and emotions I couldn't name braided and coiled into a hard knot at my chest. "I'm not certain I ever will, Won Li."

"It is enough that you do not condemn the actions or inactions of one weaker than you."

I nodded at LeBruton, trussed and lying prostrate on the paddy wagon's filthy floor. His pajama trousers were stained. Sometime during the altercation, he had soiled himself.

"What about him? To my mind, any man who'd take his fists to a woman, a dog, a horse—anything who poses no threat—is the weakest of the weak. And I sure as six kinds of hell condemn what he's done to Penelope."

Won Li smiled. "My beloved Joby. I may have misspoken to a degree, but we all have weaknesses and strengths. What I meant to impart is that Mrs. LeBruton needs your help more now than ever she has."

"If you are exacting with yourself but forgiving to others," I recited, "then you will put enmity at a distance."

"It pleases me that the lessons of the *I Ching* are familiar to you." He angled a thumb toward Jack. "Care to practice what it is you preach?"

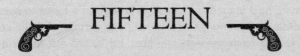

FIFTEEN

I was sitting tailor-style under the sheet of oilcloth I'd had the presence of mind to pack behind Izzy's saddle.

By the time Won Li and I had gotten home from the LeBrutons' the rain had let up and trees had even doffed the sulky droop they take on when starved for sunshine. Then wouldn't you know, I'd heard drops peck the window-glass as I'd been changing into the Union suit, itchy and still damp from the night before.

I'd hooked the neck band over an upper corner of the wardrobe, thinking it would dry faster. Perhaps it had, considering the weather, but gravity had stretched the legs clean to the floor, and the shoulder and one sleeve were pulled anti-goggling.

There'd been no help for it. About twenty feet of britches leg had been jammed into my boots, and the overlong sleeve had been yanked to my wrist. The excess girdling my arm had cocked it out like shootists depicted on covers of blood-and-thunder magazines. There'd been no help for that, either.

The previous night, I had reminded Won Li that I hadn't had much sleep of late, so I was turning in early. Out the bedroom window I'd gone to saddle Izzy and make for my hideout. If he knew I'd snuck out or in again well after midnight, he hadn't said a word.

After Jack and I exchanged apologies on the LeBrutons' lawn, he'd invited me to supper tonight. I'd failed to conjure a lie fast enough to decline. I was certain when he arrived to fetch me—shortly after I'd bailed out the window—Won Li must have called me a half dozen times before he'd rapped on my door. When I didn't answer, he might have gone as far as to open it, but a battering ram to the back wouldn't have pushed him into my room, proper.

He respected my privacy. So did I.

Crouched in my Gulliver-sized long handles under the oilcloth scrap in the pouring down rain, I pictured Won Li and Jack at the table, sipping libations and telling each other what an irresponsible, ungrateful, double-dealing, prevaricating piece of work I am.

That hurt. I cared a lot what they thought of me. Maybe I was guilty of being some of those things, some of the time, but not all of them, all of the time, and none of them without good reason, most of the time.

An upstairs light at the near corner of the house flickered, then went out. I froze, staring at the shiny, blank panes. A few moments later, my stance relaxed. Like the night before, that was the nearest thing to excitement I'd had in an hour. Could be two.

I was beginning to revise my thinking on the marvel of owning a big house. Judging by recent observations, spacious quarters spread things out too much. You'd have to be in the same room with somebody to have a conversation. And children would be neither seen nor heard. Having been one of the type that bore careful watching, the mischief I'd have made had we lived in a mansion could have wiped Ft. Smith, Arkansas, and its surrounds clean off the map.

The hair on the back of my neck quickened. I tilted my head left and closed one eye to better listen for the soft swish I'd heard behind me and to the right.

Hang it all. Either it had stopped or it had never existed but in my imagination. Oilcloth was a lousy choice of tarpaulin. Drumming raindrops blotted the noise. A wool blanket would have—

My breath hitched. There it was again. Closer. Coming steadily closer. It wasn't a cat this time. Lord God, if my heart thumped any louder, whoever it was would hear it. I turned from the waist—slowly . . . slowly. My spine locked as though the vertebrae were welded together.

Motion. A figure loomed. A wet hand clapped my mouth. Thumb and fingertips vised my jaw. I peeled my lips back. Forced my teeth apart. Chomped down on the meaty ridge below the assailant's index finger.

A muffled yowl ended with, "Shit *fire*, Joby. Turn loose—*turn loose,* damn it. It's *me.*"

The hand still at my mouth induced a heavy reliance on m-sounds. As the grip released, Jack cautioned, "Don't go to yelling or anything, all right?"

Nodding, I spied his boot inches from my bent knee. Palms together and fingers laced like a bludgeon, I swung back and clouted his big toe so hard that a ball should have shot up a stanchion and rung the brass bell at the top.

Jack squatted down beside me, teeth clenched and grimacing. "Judas priest," he whispered. "I take care not to scare you out of ten years' growth and what do I get? My hand half bit off and a broken foot."

"You thought creeping up behind me and slapping your hand over my face wouldn't scare me?"

"I was trying to keep you from screaming."

"Want to know the best way to have done that?"

"No, but I'm bound to hear it."

"How about not coming here in the first place?" I started at another window going dark. My nerves were so tight they should have pierced my skin. "How did you find me, anyway?"

"Easy." Gaze focused on the second-story windows, Jack huddled closer, pulling the oilcloth over his head. "Won Li saw you slink home last night, wet as sop. He thought you'd gone spying on the LeBrutons.

"When you came up missing tonight, I knew it wasn't them you were watching. Didn't take much to guess who it was. Spying Izzy tethered to a tree down yonder made it fact."

I shrugged. "So, now that you know, you can leave me be."

"Nope."

"This is my case, Jack."

"Your obsession, you mean." He shook his head. "I can't feature why you refuse to believe Vittorio Ciccone is a thief and a murderer."

"From the look of him, he could be both, but he didn't rob the Abercrombies and he didn't kill Belinda."

"Another hunch, huh. Keep spiking 'em this fast and you'll run out before the week does."

"It's more than a hunch." I unfolded my legs and curled

them under me. My feet were as cold and numb as paving stones. "Answer me this. Why would Ciccone climb a rope to access Belinda's bedroom from the balcony, then after he strangled her, run hell bent for election down the stairs and out the front door? And knocking over a vase on his way past?"

"He'd just killed a woman," Jack said. "He panicked."

"That's what I thought, too."

"Makes sense."

I agreed. "What doesn't is how Ciccone could knot the climbing rope around the balcony rail from the ground. Remember, there was no hook at the end of it. An amazing job of lassoing, if you ask me.

"Even if by some miracle he managed it, from all accounts Belinda was in the room when he got there. By the dressing gown she wore, she was also awake, not sleeping."

"She could have been dozing on the bed. Drowsy and unwell, but not quite ready to turn in for the night."

Papa used to brag that he could whip his weight in wildcats on four hours' sleep. Snoring to beat Billy Ned for another four or so in the rocking chair before he donned a nightshirt didn't figure into the equation.

I said, "If Belinda was dozing, the lights must have been on in the room."

"Couldn't have been, or the burglar wouldn't have risked it."

"Did you ask anyone if the room was dark or lit when Belinda's body was discovered?"

"Nope. You?"

"Never entered my mind," I said.

Jack pondered for a full minute. "If he came in and went out the front door, why'd he need a rope? Unless he tied it on to escape, if he was discovered, or the other way was blocked."

I hadn't thought of that. "Possible," I admitted, "but if it were me in a panic, I'd have wits enough to climb down from the balcony, not run pell-mell through the house."

From his expression, Jack would, too. He knew without my prompting that the vase wasn't smashed on the way in. The noise was what had wakened Jules and Pansy, and the front doors were open when he investigated. It was ludicrous to think if the burglar entered that way, he didn't close them behind him.

"Never mind entrances and exits," I said. "It's the pearl necklace that nagged at me from the start. A thief using the only fake strand of pearls Belinda owned is just too convenient." Continuing with the explanation included a fast-talking account of my second visit to the jail.

"Ah, yes. The pretty Miz Peabody with the jealous fiancé. Waylon Thomas, the turnkey, is still mooning over you." Jack chuckled. "Not that I blame him."

"You knew? And you're not angry?"

"I did and I was, but I'm not anymore." Even in ambient light, his eyes were a clear, honest blue. "You were wrong to pussyfoot around behind my back. I was wrong in acting like you need my permission to set foot out the door. If I hadn't, you wouldn't have *had* to pussyfoot."

"Well . . ." I held up a hand. "You're right. No argument. Except there's a part of me that kind of enjoys finagling my own way of doing things."

"Do tell."

"Which I'm trying to, about the pearls. Flat out, I think the robbery was faked to throw blame on the burglar. The real murderer couldn't bring himself to kill Belinda with a strand of ungodly expensive pearls."

"Himself. Meaning Hubert Abercrombie."

"Yes. Belinda was pregnant. I'll bet every dime I have that the child wasn't Hubert's. If it was, why the secrecy? Everybody from Avilla to Pansy said Belinda was nauseous after lunch. Not a soul blamed it on morning sickness, which has naught to do with time of—"

Jack squeezed my wrist. My gaze followed his. I ceased to breathe. We'd been so caught up in conversation that neither of us had seen the French doors to Belinda's balcony open.

A hooded, black-clad form knelt down to tie a rope to the wrought-iron corner post. Once secured, a coiled length was tossed over the railing.

A tickle tiptoed up my nose. I wiggled it. Pinched the bejesus out of the bridge to dam it. Eyes watery and heavy, I buried my face in Jack's shoulder.

To my throbbing eardrums, the sneeze sounded as loud as a paddle slapping water, broadside. Jack's coat must have born the brunt, for when I chanced a peek, the reverse burglar was spidering down the rope.

Jack signaled that he'd follow him, while I stayed put. No, I mouthed and pointed at myself, then him. He shook his head and peeled back his coat, displaying the revolver holstered at his hip. I shrugged and delved my boot top for my derringer. His jaw dropped, eyes slapping open as big as twin blue moons.

Without further ado, I slithered from under the oil-cloth. Crouched low, I started after the rapidly disappearing figure. Like him, I ran a zigzag pattern into and out of deep shadow. From the corner of my eye, I saw Jack doing the same, about ten feet to my left.

Neighboring homes were widely separated by weedy, vacant lots. We'd snaked through two back lawns, three, then a fourth, when I lost sight of my quarry. Hands on my knees, I squinted into the drizzly dark, trying to hear something—anything—besides the pound of my own pulse.

Jack kept going, his back hunched nigh vertical to the ground to offset his height. I started up again, praying he wasn't tracking blind. If we jogged past the burglar, he'd spot us and double back to his house.

Had Jack's arm not swung in the direction, I'd have never seen the figure climbing an ivy trellis up the wall of the sandstone-block house.

No lights showed in the back or side windows. Assuming the occupants were away, I ran for the front entrance. There was no time for niceties such as knocking. Rousing a servant, then explaining why I was there, would take too blessed long.

Into the door's keyhole, I inserted a waxed-paper-wrapped cylinder taken from the pouch strung around my neck. The tiny, explosive charge would disable the lock a lot faster than I could pick it open. Striking a match on the stone wall, I lit the short string fuse and backpedaled a safe distance.

The blast knocked me on my butt. The concussion sent me somersaulting across the wet grass, until a sizeable oak tree halted my egress. The doors fluttered by, shearing off limbs as they passed. Glass from the shattered sidelights dappled the ground like sleet.

Scrambling upright, I dashed through the smoldering maw. Acrid smoke obscured my vision. Groping and stumbling, I bashed a shin on a newel post. Screams commenced from all directions as I ran up the stairs. I burst through the door of the corner room. The burglar, silhouetted against the window, was poised to climb back out.

"Stop, thief!" I wrapped my arms around his thighs and jerked backward. We tumbled to the floor, my body bearing the brunt of both our weights. A woman shrieked, "Aaron-n-n!"

Grunting and wriggling, the burglar fought with all his might to free himself. A match flared. A bare foot kicked me in the ribs. Fingernails clawed and pinched my arms. "Let him go, you brute. Stop it, I say."

The screaming woman's English accent gave me pause. A peek at the garish, plaid pajamas smothering me from above lent a longer one. Just as I concluded that the person I'd tackled might not be the burglar, Jack bellowed my name from the doorway.

My arms fell to my sides. My captive rolled off me and leapt to his feet. Truth be known, he better resembled Izzy than Hubert Abercrombie.

Confused and mayhaps a tad disoriented by the explosion, I cocked back my head to look up at Jack. If I read his expression correctly in the scant light, he was deliberating whether the revolver he held would be put to better use dispatching me or intimidating the prisoner gripped in his other hand.

My bleary eyes averted to his captive. I blinked. Rubbed the lids with the heels of my hands. Focusing my gaze at floor level, I let it ramble upward at its own pace.

Knee-high, black, top-grain riding boots. Custom-made, judging by their fit. A pair of black riding breeches. Black silk gloves. A black cashmere sweater . . .

My eyes roved a soot-blackened face, then met Avilla Abercrombie's hateful glare.

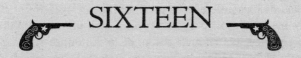

SIXTEEN

Hobbling to J. Fulton Shulteis's office the next morning, it would have taken more than a nasty cold, bruised ribs, and minor burns and cuts from flying glass to dampen my spirits. Not when I'd been right about everything viz the Abercrombie case.

Well, everything except the perpetrator and the motive.

My original and favorite suspects, the elusive Gertrude Hiss and Sam Merck, had been joined in holy wedlock an hour before Belinda Abercrombie's funeral. When they'd arrived at the manse the night of the murder, Merck was terrified he'd be accused of the crime. He'd served two years in prison for assault and petty larceny and was certain to be a suspect.

Gert guaranteed it by vowing she'd summon a constable to arrest him, then testify for the prosecution if Sam didn't marry her. A justice of the peace in Salida had officiated the next day.

Sam might not have been a beaming bridegroom, but if he enjoyed German cuisine, starvation would be the least of his worries.

After being startled by the explosion and fall from the trellis into Jack's arms, Avilla had little choice but to confess. That, and him finding the pillow slip full of Belinda's jewels tucked in the hollow posts of Avilla's canopy bed.

The child her stepmother was carrying was Hubert's. Belinda had suffered two previous miscarriages, thus had sworn her husband to secrecy until such time she felt the pregnancy was enough advanced to announce it. Naturally, Hubert had told Avilla, then extracted a promise that she'd act surprised when Belinda disclosed the happy news.

Jack and I shared our suspicions about the earlier miscarriages, but Avilla denied doing anything to cause them. Perhaps she hadn't. She was dead-bang guilty of one murder, and like Papa always said, "You can only hang once."

Money was the motive. With the fifty-fifty chance that Avilla's half sibling would be male, upon Belinda's death the child would inherit the entire estate, as Hubert ascribed to the old-fashioned notion that daughters should marry well and sons should carry on the family name and business.

Had the baby been female, Avilla's inheritance would have been halved—assuming, as she didn't, that Belinda didn't fritter away every nickel before Avilla got a crack at it. Ridding herself of Belinda and unborn brother or sister ensured Avilla's future as a very wealthy young woman.

The modus operandi was simple, although it required patience, then near-perfect timing. When Belinda was too queasy for dinner at the Estabrooks, Avilla slipped a sleeping draught into Hubert's drink before they went upstairs for the reading.

When Hubert nodded off, Avilla went to Belinda's room and told her Hubert was ill. When Belinda rose to check on him, Avilla strangled her with the imitation pearls taken in advance from the jewel case. Avilla emptied the case into a pillow slip, stashed it temporarily in the back of her wardrobe, returned to affix the rope to the balcony rail, then hastened downstairs to open the doors and knock the vase off the table to waken the servants.

I'd also been slightly mistaken about the nature of the bruise on Hubert's hand. I thought he'd barked it on the railing while tying the "burglar's" rope. In reality, it was the mark left by Avilla's thumb when she pressured the same point on Hubert's hand to rouse him as Won Li did to banish my headaches.

Such was an example of yin and yang. Gentle pressure on specific points all over the body had curative properties. A hard gouge effected pain ranging from mild discomfort to excruciating.

Avilla's sole mistake, which murderers almost always make, was to gild the lily. Bumping into a scraggly stranger on the street—namely, Vittorio Ciccone—and dropping the bar-pin in his pocket was brilliant. What down-on-his-luck drifter wouldn't believe it to be manna from heaven and cash in on his luck?

Avilla must have danced a merry jig when she heard that the postmaster had identified Ciccone as having mailed a mystery parcel before he attempted to pawn the jewelry.

When the constables delivered Ciccone to his door not an hour after Garret McCoyne's assistant posted the reward flyer, greed entrapped the postmaster. A share of the bounty offered for information and ridding the city of a derelict non-Caucasian appealed to his bigoted attitude. He was subsequently arrested for bearing false witness in a homicide investigation.

When Avilla later heard that Ciccone had been released from jail, she decided the Ladykiller Thief must strike again. In doing so, she overplayed what might well have been a pat hand.

Like liars parlay too much information, criminals of all kinds tend to cover and recover their tracks with boulders when laying low would hide them sufficiently.

Because she had, I manufactured a reasonably fair excuse to explain to Aaron and Geneva Wilhelm-Oglethorpe why I'd blown the doors off their house and wrestled Aaron to the floor when he'd gone to the window to investigate the presumed earthquake.

"I think you'll agree that Avilla Abercrombie is not of sound mind," I'd said.

The Wilhelm-Oglethorpes had exchanged a glance I'd interpreted as meaning my sanity was equally fragile. "We'll never know whether Avilla's scheme to re-frame Vittorio Ciccone would have extended to another murder."

Geneva gasped. "You mean . . ."

"It's possible." I splayed my hands. "I'm not saying this to frighten you after the fact. It just seems common sense that if Belinda Abercrombie was thought to have been killed during the commission of a burglary, Avilla would not have deviated from that theory."

Aaron clutched his wife's arm. "Did you hear that, Geneva? Great God, we came a whisker from being slain in our beds tonight."

"True enough, but . . ." Geneva frowned up at me. "Was

it necessary to dynamite a huge, smoldering hole in the front of our house to prevent it?"

Dynamite was not the pyrotechnic I'd used, but I refrained from correcting her. "I really can't say for certain, Mrs. Wilhelm-Oglethorpe. I am sincerely sorry for the damage, but might I point out, it was the concussion that prevented Avilla from entering through the window."

"Yes, yes 'twas," Aaron said. "The constable caught her on the way down."

"From my position at the front of the house," I went on, "I had no idea that she was already in custody. An argument could be waged that she wouldn't have time to murder both of you, before your butler answered my knock, but . . ."

Aaron said, "If she'd only got one of us, it would have been you, pet. You sleep nearer the window."

"I beg your pardon. You snore so loudly, surely she'd have slit your throat first for the tranquility it afforded."

"That's a horrible thing to say. Positively macabre."

"It's the truth."

"Not."

" 'Tis, too."

Before the spat escalated further, I apologized again for the damages. Thinking it would enhance my sincerity, I then offered to pay for them.

Geneva accepted with alacrity. Aaron argued that their lives were more valuable than a couple of doors and sidelights, even though they'd been imported from Wales at no small expense.

Geneva suggested I reimburse their cost and leave the balance of the repairs to them. "Five thousand will cover it, I should think."

"*Dollars?*"

"That is a bit excessive, love, don't you think? After all, we do owe our lives to Miss Sawyer." He beamed up at me. "Make it two thousand and we'll call it square."

The air whooshed from my lungs. I grabbed the edge of a console to keep from fainting dead away.

"Four thousand," Geneva yelped.

"Three!"

"Twenty-five hundred," she said. "That's my final offer, Aaron. Take it or leave it."

Two hours later, we settled on five hundred, payable in installments for the rest of my natural life.

Won Li said I'd gotten off easy. I told him if I heard another word about it, I'd cut off his pigtail and put it where the sun don't shine.

Percy wasn't at his desk when I entered J. Fulton Shulteis's office to collect the much-needed fee for the LeBruton case. In a peculiar way, the clerk's absence was a disappointment. I made a mental note to make up for it, next visit.

The enthusiasm with which Fulton greeted me had me glancing over my shoulder to see if, say, Queen Victoria herself were standing in my shadow.

"Allow me to add my congratulations to the multitudes for a job well done." He grinned around a fat cigar that looked entirely too much like a similarly brown, elongated object. The other hand held up the newspaper. Just like the copy I bought that morning, the headline read "Joe B. Sawyer Captures Killer."

Jack was quoted as crediting me and Sawyer Investigations with contributing to Avilla Abercrombie's arrest. Alas, the tin-eared reporter heard the name as "Joe B.," not Joby. A correction was to be printed in tomorrow's edition, but the squib would likely appear between advertisements for magnetized trusses and bunion pads.

Shulteis said, "According to the account, your father couldn't have solved Belinda Abercrombie's murder without your help. Nor dispensing with LeBruton, for that matter."

On the surface, they were true statements. But criminitlies, was I weary of Papa's posthumous reputation eclipsing mine.

Fulton said, "So, the police think the real thief must have skipped town, when news of the murder got out, eh?"

"They do?"

"That's what the paper says. Took the loot from the McCoynes and Whitelaws and vamoosed." Pages rustled, then he pointed at a small piece below the third's fold. "Wouldn't have done him much good to stay in the city. To risk apprehension while burgling another house was an invitation to a murder charge."

The thief getting away scot-free irked my sense of justice and destroyed my bank account. Refunding the victims' retainer would be my next errand. Wise of me not to spend any of the advance, but I'd had hopes of earning a goodly piece of it. All told, between the damages incurred, expenses unretrievable, and returning the hundred-dollar bank draft, I'd need a loan to buy a bottle of red ink with which to update the agency's ledger.

I prayed the fee I'd come to collect would cover the rents due. And force a sense of satisfaction at the high odds of the burglar getting caught someday. I smiled to myself. Maybe even by me.

"I, uh, don't mean to rush you, Joby, but I do have to be at the courthouse in a quarter hour."

"Something to do with the LeBruton dissolution, I hope?"

"No dissolution needed. The rake is a bigamist, three times over. Penelope's under a doctor's care for malaise and attending symptoms of depression, but in time, she'll be all right."

With Abelia's help, I thought she likely would.

Fulton tapped a sheaf of papers on his desk. "So, Joby. Congratulations, again, and rest assured, I will enlist the services of Sawyer Investigations at the soonest opportunity."

"Thank you, Fulton. For the praise and the promise."

"You're very welcome."

I hesitated a moment, then added, "But aren't you forgetting something?"

"No . . . No, I don't believe so."

Shyster, I thought. The nickname wasn't ill deserved. "The fee. For the LeBruton case. Dissolution or no, I believe the agency is deserving of a fee for services rendered."

He laughed. "Well, you're a little too late to collect it."

My heart stopped, then ricocheted wildly in my chest. "What do you mean, too late?"

Shulteis lofted a box of imported cigars. "I finally had the bona fide pleasure of making your father's acquaintance, my dear. Lo, we had the most marvelous chat. What a storyteller he is. And what a repertoire of blood-and-thunder stories he has to tell."

He chuckled, as though recalling an exquisitely bawdy anecdote featuring a cast of buxom Jezebels. "Naturally, when Joe said he must be going and inquired after the fee, I was more than happy to oblige."

The body contains approximately eight quarts of blood.

As God is my witness, both gallons drained from mine and puddled at my ankles.

As the room faded from a sickly ochre to gray-black, I heard Shulteis say, "Truth be known, I should have doubled the payment for the honor of shaking a genuine hero's hand."

POCKET BOOKS
PROUDLY PRESENTS

A LADY NEVER MEDDLES IN MURDER

SUZANN LEDBETTER

Available January 2004
from Pocket Books

Turn the page for a preview of
A Lady Never Meddles in Murder. . . .

"I have never fainted, not once in my entire twenty-two years, and I'll thank you never to accuse me of it again."

The statement was a tad brassy for a young woman who'd just regained consciousness on the carpeted floor of J. Fulton Shulteis's law office. Then again, being told that my father had resurrected himself from the grave to collect the fee owed the detective agency established in his name should qualify as an extenuating circumstance.

To be fair, Fulton's pronouncement had been neither as boorish or blunt as implied. Not that he wasn't given to both on occasion. The most vivid example was the lecture he delivered at the Denver City jail after my arrest for lewd and lascivious behavior. Though I was dancing the cancan atop the bar when the police raided Madame Felicity's sporting house, my objective was to get the goods on the adulterous spouse of one of Fulton's clients.

Nor could I fault the delight he'd expressed at finally having met the elusive, illustrious Deputy U.S. Marshal Joseph Beckworth Sawyer. Papa's renown as a lawman had traveled from the Arkansas Western District to Colorado Territory well before he resigned his commission to become a private investigator.

Why, just this morning, the *Rocky Mountain News* spared no adjectives in praising Papa's capture of a murderer, plus a suspected one and bigamist wanted in three states. The feat was most worthy of notoriety, particularly for a man who'd suffered a fatal heart attack six months ago, en route to Denver City.

Mine wrenched all over again, thinking of my father swaddled in a tattered blanket to sleep for eternity near a desolate wagon road in southwest Kansas. My Chinese patron, Won Li, and I had no choice but to inter Papa where he'd fallen. A man of his courage and devotion to justice deserved a bronze monument to his memory. For him to rest beneath a rude cross graven with his name for a tombstone was a tick short of infamy.

Leaving nothing behind in Fort Smith to return to, Won Li and I had soldiered on to Colorado's territorial capitol. Once there, I could have hired on as a shopgirl to earn our keep, had I the slightest inclination toward hawking ladies' underdrawers, or tins of Newton's Heave, Cough, Distemper, and Indigestion compound. My sights could also have set on schoolteaching, had self-educated expertise in botany, anatomy, chemistry, herbology, criminalistics, and pyrotechnics been in demand.

Instead, I founded the detective agency in Papa's name—traded on it, as Won Li opined. He's right, I suppose, but with or without a mouthful of a handle like Josephine Beckworth Sawyer, pigs would fly before a client would knowingly employed a female to investigate sundry crimes and misdemeanors.

To excuse the official proprietor's chronic absences, I alluded to Papa's dyspeptic stomach, bouts of catarrh, frequent sojourns from the city pursuant to his caseload, and the ever-dependable, "Sorry, but Mr. Sawyer just stepped out a moment ago."

This tangled web of deceit was of my own weave, but there was no *quid pro quo* in a miscreant capitalizing on Papa's name and reputation, much less in stealing the fee owed me for freeing a belle from the bonds and fists of unholy matrimony. The son of a she-dog who had, would rue the day he concocted his scheme. Hell hath no fury like a woman scorned, but a special corner of Hades is reserved for those of us whelped and reared in the wilds of darkest Arkansas.

Fulton reached down a flabby hand to me, which I accepted. A chemise, corset, petticoats and a nipped-waist dress hardly allow for proper respiration. To indulge in an acrobatic maneuver might dislodge a rib, or an organ of import, such as my spleen.

I said, "It was a carpet wrinkle that tripped my feet. If I were you, I'd have it stretched and relaid at my earliest convenience."

He surveyed the fern- and ivy-patterned expanse surrounding the visitor's chair I'd gripped the back of, before landing flat of my own. "Wrinkles? I don't see any wrinkles."

"Neither did I, until I fell victim to one."

Moving sideward, Fulton studied my face, then frowned. "Egad, Joby. That bruise on your cheek—"

"Is nothing." I sidled away from scrutiny. "I ran into a door last night."

Actually, a door ran into me. Two towering and quite solid ones to be exact, along with the leaded glass sidelights gracing Aaron and Geneva Wilhelm-Oglethorpe's stately home. The nitrostarch admixture I'd applied to disable the locks accomplished its purpose, but blowing the mansion's entryway to flinders in the process wasn't part of the original plan.

The owners and I eventually bargained down the damages from five thousand dollars to five hundred. The sum was payable in installments I'd bequeath my heirs, assuming I ever produced any.

I again reassured Fulton that I wasn't injured in the physical sense. It was the one sustained by my empty coin purse and bank account that could prove fatal to Sawyer Investigations. No business could survive without capital. The money paid in good faith to the bogus Joseph Beckworth Sawyer wouldn't have retired my numerous debts, but no income whatsoever sank me so far in the hole, I'd need ladders and a long rope to glimpse blue sky.

Barring a stampede clamoring to hire the agency's services, my only recourse was to apprehend the thief and recover the purloined cash. Complicating that solution was the fact I had no earthly idea what the man looked like. Nor could I ask Fulton outright for a description. One presumes a daughter in command of her faculties needn't ask after her father's height, build, hair color, distinguishing scars, and manner of dress.

Fortunately, I became adept at contrivance at a tender age and practiced it as regularly as a pianist would a Chopin etude. "At breakfast," I said, "Papa promised his first order of the day would be a haircut and a shave. Was the Joe B. Sawyer who called on you of the shorn persuasion, or still as shaggy as a mountain goat?"

Fulton chuckled as he rounded his desk. A satchel and bowler were retrieved in preparation for a court hearing he'd mentioned earlier. "The comparison might be apt, but somewhat disrespectful, don't you think?"

Wherever Papa's soul had found rest, he knew bunkum when he heard it. Also the truth. From Fulton's rebuke, I surmised that the imposter was also estranged from the tonsorial arts. The clue narrowed my field of suspects to approximately seventy-five percent of Denver City's male population.

Alas, even if I bamboozled Fulton into a chapter and verse portrait, unless the charlatan had a clubfoot and a glass eye, such information is almost always too general for good use. I daresay the city's boardwalks don't teem with slender, shapely young ladies with black hair and olive complexions, yet my attributes are not unique.

Still, I had to try. The agency's future depended on it.

The real Joe B. Sawyer had stood a full six-foot-three in his socks. J. Fulton Shulteis was a couple of inches shorter than me—the lifts in his shoes notwithstanding. I begged the law of averages to find in my favor, then said, "Disrespect had naught to do with my analogy. I'm sure you'll agree, a well-groomed man of Papa's size would inspire confidence in prospective clients and be no less intimidating to scofflaws."

Fulton opened the office door for our departure. "I'll grant, Sawyer is a great bear of a chap, but knowing his daughter as I do, I'd wager he is, at this very moment, wedged into a barber's chair and praying he'll depart it with both ears intact."

Strolling from his sumptuous inner sanctum to the reception area unfolded like a scene from a Dickens novel. The cramped space was drafty in winter and steamy in summer. The walls were plastered, but the floor was bare wood and the unoccupied desk chair listed severely to starboard. The office of Sawyer Investigations was hardly prepossessing, but in comparison, this ground-level garret had all the ambience of an oversized outhouse.

Percy, Fulton's cadaverous clerk, was still away from his post. Being as much an accoutrement as the globed coal-oil lamp at the desk's far corner, I asked if the poor lad had taken ill.

"No, I'd say he's somewhere between the bank and the newspaper office, picking up the new stationery we ordered." The tip of the attorney's hat revealed the ornery glint in his eye. "I'll be sure to pass on your concern, though. Percy will be elated to hear of it."

An exaggeration, if ever there was one. The clerk and I weren't enemies, but assuredly weren't friends. The root of our coexistence was to annoy the bejesus out of each other. I should be ashamed of myself for taking pleasure in besting Percy at every opportunity, but everyone knows at least one other who doesn't have sense enough to hush when he's behind.

Fulton and I exchanged farewells, then he hoisted his roly-poly frame into a surrey hired to transport him to his appointment. The springs chirruped melodiously as the driver gidapped the unmatched team for the six-block journey.

It wasn't much farther to my next errand, but in my present mood, the distance seemed equal to Moses' expedition from Goshen.

Weekend rains had slaked August's drought and thrown off its sultry cloak. It was a welcome respite, but exacted a toll on horses and humans consigned to thoroughfares resembling a ruddy clay and manure-clodded stew. Soon, the incessant wind would dry the stenchy wallow to corduroyed cement.

I hugged my reticule, flummoxed by how a morning that dawned triumphant had turned on me like a fierce dog. The litany of *couldn'ts* drumming in my head echoed the stamp of my high-laced shoes on the boardwalk.

First off, the imposter's ruse couldn't be reported to the police. In my experience, law enforcement takes a dim view of complainants guilty of fraud raising Billy Ned about another's petty larceny. The attitude reflects George Herbert's "Whose house is of glass, must not throw stones at another." Countering it with John 8:7, "He that is without sin among you, let him first cast a stone," would cut no mustard with the cops.

Above all, I couldn't compromise Constable Jack O'Shaughnessy's blissful ignorance of the situation. Lies of the number and magnitude I'd told him might imply a significant lack of faith in a man I liked enormously and might even love. Verily, I trusted Jack second to Won Li. It was just that the proper moment to confess the hoax I'd perpetrated on my beau and the entire town hadn't arisen as yet.

Which left the only female detective west of the Mississippi to her own devices. What, precisely, they might be and how I'd institute them, I couldn't fathom.

The false-fronted brick building I sought on Arapahoe Street between G and H was as nondescript as its owner, Avery Whitelaw. He and a business associate, Garret McCoyne, had solicited the agency's help in recovering a trove of precious jewels recently burgled from their respective homes.

I spied my quarry near the end of the block. He'd secured a pasteboard carton of rolled maps in the bed of a buckboard and was preparing to leave. "Mr. Whitelaw," I called. When he failed to acknowledge me, I lodged a thumb and pinky finger between my teeth and whistled like a teamster.

In unison, Whitelaw's horse, saddled mounts hitched to the rail, and others passing on the street pricked their ears, reared their heads, and stutter-stepped. A rider hand-rolling a cigarette lurched sideways, then tumbled off, butt over boot soles. The pond of a puddle he landed in cushioned his fall, but his suddenly unencumbered dun mare bucked and sunfished, her hooves firing mud like twin shotgun barrels.

Bystanders didn't connect the incitement to riot with the innocent-looking young brunette in the hideous, flower-fraught hat. I added another impetuosity to the thousands for which I'd beg atonement on my deathbed, then greeted Avery Whitelaw like a lady.

"Miss Sawyer." He smiled and swept off a wide-brimmed John B. "What a lovely surprise."

From my reticule I removed a sealed envelope containing a hundred-dollar bank note. "With my sincerest apologies, I'm returning the retainer you and Mr. Mc-Coyne paid the agency last week."

"You're quitting the case?"

'There is no case to pursue, sir. I must agree with the police that your jewelry won't be found in Denver City. It was probably smuggled out shortly after the burglaries, and days before you hired me."

Nodding, Whitelaw took the envelope as though it was advance notice from the Grim Reaper. "I figured as much, but hoped I was wrong." He sucked his teeth and sighed. "The heirlooms were irreplaceable. Oh, how I dread telling my wife they're gone for good."

"Perhaps not," I blurted, out of sympathy for and empathy with his plight. Unlike Garret McCoyne, the mining entrepreneur had treated me as an equal, not a maid of all work. "It stands to reason, a collection as valuable as yours and the McCoynes' would be fenced in a larger city. New York, most definitely, followed by San Francisco, or Chicago.

"While it might be for naught, I'd suggest you write the Pinkerton National Detective Agency and enclose a list and description of the pieces—in particular, those of unusual design or antiquity. Pinkerton's services don't come cheap, but he has the resources and an army of operatives to assist in the search."

Whitelaw's face brightened. Repeating my caution didn't dull it one iota. He insisted on giving me five dollars for my time and astute advice. Accepting it increased my net worth a hundred-percent.

Four-bits of his largess was squandered on coffee and pastries at the Mountain Home Coffeehouse and Confectionery. Glover Rudd, a reporter for the *Rocky Mountain News*, had sent a note requesting a meeting at the wondrously aromatic establishment. I didn't know what compelled Rudd's invitation, but as soon as he arrived, I'd ask that he listen sharp in the future for the distinction between Joe B. Sawyer and Joby Sawyer—short for my unwieldy Christian name.

I didn't begrudge Papa the laurels Rudd mistakenly heaped on him in print this morning. The banner headlined feature was far more beneficial to Sawyer Investigations than a boxed advertisement inserted between one for fancy sewing—a euphemism for prostitution—and another heralding the latest advance in magnetic vigor restoratives—a euphemism for impotency cures. Whether ascribable to newspaper editors' senses of humor or irony, the two neighbored each other more often than not.

An hour later, I concluded that bordertown ruffians had superior manners to members of the fourth estate. I left the coffeehouse in a huff, vowing to post a bill for my delicious, but extravagant snack to Mr. Rudd as soon as I reached the office.

Rare had been days when, in retrospect, getting out of bed had seemed like an act of valor. It was a sore temptation to chuck the remainder of this one and go home, crawl back under the covers and pull them over my head.

What stopped me was the inevitability of Won Li's disapproval. It would be expressed with a quote from Confucius criticizing the luxury of sleep in the daytime, unless one is a victim of a debilitating illness or one's demise is either imminent or has already occurred.

"Good people nurture character with fruitful action," my patron would intone, with the haughty scowl only those of Asian extraction can produce. "Rotten wood cannot be sculpted, a manure wall cannot be plastered."

Astonishing though it may be, in twelve years, I'd yet to devise a sufficiently clever retort to that philosophy.

Had I guessed that being gulled, robbed, and stood up at the coffeehouse would rank as the high points of my day, I'd have gladly risked Won Li's reproach.

Visit the
Simon & Schuster Web site:
www.SimonSays.com

and sign up for our
mystery e-mail updates!

Keep up on the latest
new releases, author appearances,
news, chats, special offers, and more!
We'll deliver the information
right to your inbox — if it's new,
you'll know about it.

SIMON & SCHUSTER
A VIACOM COMPANY
www.SimonSays.com

POCKET BOOKS

POCKET STAR BOOKS